THE HONEST FISHERMAN
AND OTHER STORIES

By MAURICE WALSH

THE
HONEST FISHERMAN
AND OTHER STORIES

BY

MAURICE WALSH

W. & R. CHAMBERS, LTD.
LONDON AND EDINBURGH

First Impression 1954

F

128854

All the characters and events in this book are fictitious,
and no reference is made inadvertently to any living
person, by name, implication, or description

Printed in Great Britain
by T. and A. CONSTABLE LTD., Hopetoun Street,
Printers to the University of Edinburgh

CONTENTS

THE HONEST FISHERMAN

LISTEN to me now! I am an honestogod angler. That is, I am as honest an angler as any angler ever is—or can be. I might, to suit a story or an occasion, add an ounce or, maybe, two to the weight of a fish I had landed—or lost, as the case might be, and by fish I mean salmon and nothing else but that king of running water; but, and remember my words, I am not addicted to nefarious methods by long-handled gaff, or treble-hook, or wire-loop, or bagnet, or murderous gelignite, or all the other evil usages that tempt greedy men. Though, mind you, I know something about these same methods, and well I ought, for I am acquainted of many otherwise honest men who, by dint of circumstance, are not as guiltless as they pretend.

The Village—that is what I am calling it for particular reasons—straggled its thatched and slated houses up the beech-grown and furzy slope from the Ullachowen River; and for three miles down and four up the Ullachowen linked some of the finest salmon-reaches in all Kerry. Kerry is wide, high, and handsome, and you can put your finger on The Village and The River, if you are able. You have it? Good man, yourself!

From March on to August The Village, outside working hours, did nothing else but think and talk and breathe and live and catch and, sometimes, eat salmon. Begod, sir! Some of us looked like salmon,

7

wise and all that we were. And where most of the
talking was done was in Michael Danny's flagged
kitchen. Michael Danny! You know him? Why not
you, and you looking at him this minute?

Yes, sir! In my kitchen. In the dark of the spring
evenings, in the dusk of the summer nights, when the
lamp was lit and the light shining on the dresser of
delf and glistening on the black rafters, 'with a fine
turf fire and the hearth swept clane,' as the song says—
but in them days there was no baby in the cradle nor
no wife to wet the tay, for I was a bachelor man not
accustomated to the female gender—in the gloaming
and the dark a gathering of the lads, some of them
twenty years old and more of them seventy years
young, used gather in my kitchen, sitting about on the
home-made chairs and on the bed-settle against the
wall, smoking at their ease and directing an odd spit
in the general direction of the fire, poking fun here and
there, and talking, talking, talking. And the talk
was salmon, all salmon: how a salmon was caught,
and how a salmon was lost, and where a good fish
lay in a pool, and how it moved morning or evening,
and the weight and length and girth of it approximate,
and what it might take, and what it would not take,
and what it would damwell have to take if the occasion
demanded.

Mind you, we were not rogue fishermen by habit—
I never was, and that is well known—but if the water
was low and stale, and the wind from the east, and
the sky brass, and if a fish was needed for a wedding or
a christening or a priest's dinner, or for a friend in
Dublin, or for this or that, a fish was stalked and a

8

fish was landed, and no harm done. On my solemn word, we were a prudent assortment of sound anglers, dead against wholesale slaughter, and reasonably careful to preserve the water for ourselves and our friends and the two fishing-hotels that profited The Village and The County. Now I'll tell my story.

Everything was going nice and easy and circumspect and give-and-take till a certain March not so long ago; and then we got a wallop in the wind that did not leave us a stem of our senses for three endless weeks.

It was a bitter, withering March, clear and calm and frosty, with an east drift of air day and night, and there had not been a drop of soft rain for six weeks—the only rain that will make a fish live and ready. The fish were in the pools, as we well knew, but what use was that when devil a fish would as much as look at a fly or a minnow or even a fat worm slipped over a ledge in the fall of the evening. In pure derision the silver beauties would curve over your very leader trailing in the water, but not one of them would give that head-and-tail rise of a fish on the take. So if a lad wanted a fish for a particular purpose what could he do but what he had to do?

We did not complain—not to any great extent. Sure there was a long season before us; a spate of rain would come some day, any day; the waiting fish would go upstream to the spawning beds; and a new game lot would come in over the bar from the estuary. So we behaved ourselves in a more or less continent sort of way, and did no more than curse the weather mildly.

And then came a certain evening. I was sitting at

my own fireside, but the cheerful fire of turf and bog-
pine had no cheer for me. The dusk was deepening,
but I did not put a match to the lamp, for the blaze of
resined roots, dancing shadows on walls and dresser,
gave light enough, and, anyway, I hadn't the heart
for more illumination. I hadn't the heart even to light
a soothing pipe. I just sat staring gloomily into the
red of the fire and seeing strange molten valleys and
broken towers flaming.

After a while the latch lifted, and old Tom Roddy
drifted in, a decent man and the soundest angler in our
school, though I could put another man first if I wanted
to.

'God save all here!' he murmured the usual salute.

'God save you kindly!' I gave back. 'Pull your
chair in.'

He sat over against me, and drew a long breath.
Usually, like myself, he would be smoking like a kiln,
but to-night he had his pipe in his hand, and it was
empty. After a while he said in a pained sort of
way:

'Don't tell me 'tis true, Michael Danny?'

'If what's in my mind is in your mind, 'tis too dam'
true,' I told him.

'We are ruinated so,' said he.

'Pole-axed,' said I.

'Hamstrung,' said he.

'Hog-tied and quartered,' said I.

We left it at that, and went on looking into the fire
in ignoble silence.

The latch lifted again and two more of the school
came in, and two more after that, and then one by

one, until the full company was assembled, slumped about on the chairs and settle-bed, and not as much as a glum word out of them. But the feeling of bad temper and worse humour you could cut with a knife.

''Tis the truth,' said Tom Roddy at last. 'Michael Danny says so.'

'The man is married to my own niece, and that makes it worse,' I said.

Young Eamon Broder, the mouthpiece of the juniors, lifted his voice in bitterness.

'There was no blood spilt in The Village since the Troubled Days. It is time we turned a new leaf.'

'None of that,' I said sharply. 'The bad days are gone forever, and this misfortunate thing will right itself.'

'It is up to you if it doesn't, seeing that you are his wife's uncle,' said young Broder meaningly.

'Blast your eyes!' I began to storm, but there the door opened, and in stepped the man who was in all our minds.

You could hear the long draw of breath, like the sough of a wave, go back and fore across the room. But no one answered the formal salute, and no one moved except Eamon Broder, who drew his feet back and leant forward in his chair like a tiger ready to pounce.

The incomer stood wide-legged in the middle of the floor and looked around him. The blaze from the fire showed the whites of his eyes, made his cheekbones stand out above the hollows below, and outlined the prow of his long, obstinate jaw. He was not a cowardly man, whatever else he was.

His name was Dan Casson, a lank, black-browed, slab-sided son of a gun, with not a trace of humour or wit in him. His people came from the east of Limerick but he had lived in The Village for a matter of ten years, and, as I said, was husband to my own niece, the Lord forgive her. He was not a quarrelsome man, I'll say that for him, but as he stood there in my kitchen he was in danger of strangulation by several eager hands.

All the chairs were occupied, but there was room on the settle if a couple of the boys moved over. They did not, and he noted that, and nodded his lean head.

'I see that the news has spread,' he said in his rumble of a voice, 'and I am here to make sure that ye got it right. Are ye listening to me?'

No one answered him. He was no talker, Dan Casson, but to-night the right words came out of his mouth.

'Are ye listening to me?' he said. 'I have a wife and three kids, and I wanted a job, and a good job, and a job that pleased me down to the ground, and that job I applied for, and that job I got. Are ye listening? Ye are. By this morning's post the Fishing Conservators appointed me River Warden over seven miles of the Ullachowen, three down and four up.' He tapped his flat chest. 'Take a look at me! I am the new Warden.'

And that was the terrible thing that had dumbfounded all of us. We would not, and never did, mind a river warden from outside the community. He would do his duty as he saw it, and we would play the game with him as the cards lay. But a man of The

Village turning on us, that was a disaster to bring down thunder and lightning and heavy showers.

But there was worse to it than that. Dan Casson had a terrible honest streak in him, and was cursed with a conscience that wouldn't allow the sound flesh to grow on his bones. He loved fish, but he would not take a salmon rod into his two hands because it might lead him into temptation, for he held with might and main that it was a mortal sin to take a fish out of the water except by the ways laid down by the Fishing Conservators as by Law appointed. Begod, sir! in his mind the Conservators were second only to the Deity, the Lord forgive him! Did you ever hear the like?

He loved fish and their ways, as I said, and in his spare time, in the long evenings and Saturday afternoons and all Sundays, you would encounter him up and down the river banks, observing this and that, noting the lie of a fish, talking with an angler here and there, watching how a fish was landed, and protesting with indignation if the occasion demanded it. And now he was river warden with power in his hands.

But there was worse still. Dan Casson knew us to marrow of our bones. He liked to be where fish was talked, and you would find him in my kitchen most nights of the week, not a word out of him, but his ears open, and his memory holding everything like a sticking plaster. He knew what we would do, and what we would not do, in certain circumstances, how we would set out to do a thing, the pools we'd choose, and every dam' thing in the process of landing a fish one way or another. We could no longer call our souls our own.

That was our new river warden, stubborn as a mule in righteousness. But like all stubborn men he had his weak point: he was thin-skinned, and hated to be ridiculed. You did not know that about stubborn men? No! And I want you to remember it. His wife told me, and asked me to stop the lads making fun of his asininity. I didn't, of course, for an Irishman will make fun of the Devil himself, or a bishop even. And so a bit of resentment was smouldering in Dan, and he wouldn't mind using his teeth if he got a chance.

He stood there now, and he knew that he had us in the heel of his fist, and he knew that we knew it, and that was a salve to his thin skin. But he made a small mistake in rubbing salt into us, for he went on talking. He threw his hands wide.

'I know the reaches of the Ullachowen like the palm of that hand, and I know ye, every man-jack, like the palm of that one. I'll do my job fair and square and above-board, day and dark, morning-noon-and-night, rain or shine, and I warn ye now that if I catch any scoundrel taking a fish by illegal method I'll put a plaster on him to hold him down till Lady Day in Harvest. And listen! I know I'll catch some of ye, for ye have the bad drop in ye, and I know the source it came out of.'

And there he thrust his long head in my direction and went on.

'I am talking to you, Michael Danny, you ould fox, pretending butter wouldn't melt in your mouth. You are my wife's uncle, but you are the man I'll be watching particular and constant. And I'll get you,

and I'll get you so good and hard that you'll be a
lesson to all these young shavers, and you leading them
into evil ways. That's all now, and good-night to
ye? By the powers! that was a speech to the tried
and condemned.

He turned on his heel, flung the door wide, and left
us to chew the cud. In two jumps I banged the door
shut, drove the bolt home, and set my back against it.
Three or four of the youngsters were on their feet,
eager for action, and their sort of action would be hell
and damnation for all of us.

'Take it easy!' I lifted my voice over the hullabaloo.
'No one was ever hung out of The Village.'

'The Village is finished,' cried a young fellow.

'Let us break a leg on him,' proposed Eamon Broder,
'and that'll hold him for three months anyway.'

I had to do the holding now or never. I lifted my
two hands, and Tom Roddy added his voice to mine;
and after a while they listened to me.

'You heard him,' I said, 'and don't forget he is
connected with my family. It was me he challenged,
though he had small right, and I never turned down a
challenge from any man, and I won't now. Dan
Casson will break me or I'll break him, and I will have
no man interfere between us. Do you hear?'

'How long do you want?' Eamon the firebrand
wanted to know.

'Give me till the weather breaks,' I said without
thinking. 'After that he can't hurt us, and we fishing
decently for fish on the take.'

'That might be the middle of May,' someone
protested.

Tom Roddy came to my aid again, and we made them see reason at last; and after an hour I let them go homewards in peaceful gloom.

That night I prayed hard and long for rain, for I hadn't the least notion how to circumvent a man of Dan Casson's narrow honesty and unnatural virtue. But what was the use of praying for rain and soft skies with the wind where it was, north of east?

As you may remember, that dry cold spell of weather did not break till the middle of April, and long before that the fat was in the fire, for our traitor warden caught two of the venturesome lads red-handed, a fish on the gaff and no hook in its mouth. And the fine clapped on them by the District Justice just about broke us, for, of course, we had to send the hat round to save a jail sentence.

It was then I saw the writing on the wall, for I caught members of our school throwing strange and doubtful glances in my direction, and, one by one, they gave up their nightly meetings in my kitchen. After all, I was Dan Casson's wife's uncle, and why should I do anything to deprive him of his job? It was as plain as the nose on my face that something would have to be done promptly, and that I was the dam' fool who had to do it.

So I went into a committee and conference of one, and looked at the writing on the wall for an hour, and then another—No! At the end of an hour and a half my guardian angel—or was it?—put a thought into my head: I remembered Dan Casson's thin-skinnedness.

I contemplated that thin-skinnedness for another

hour, for it was clear to me that the only way of getting at Dan Casson was by ridiculing him; and at the end of the hour I thought I saw a chance I could take; a mighty slim chance, and it might land me in a hole not easy to get out of; but there was nothing else under the sky that offered itself. I decided to take that chance, and I'll tell you what I did.

On a certain day I slipped up to Limerick City, fifty miles away, and no one saw me go. There I saw a friend closer to me than a brother, and I put the case before him. He was an angler himself, and he saw my difficulty, and he agreed that something must be done, and he was agreeable as to what should be done.

'Go home, you vagabond!' said he, 'and if the worst comes to the worst I'll meet you in jail.'

So I went home, and two days later on a certain morning I got up bright and early, and to the Devil with breakfast! I stuck my feet into rubber gum-boots that didn't leak in more than two places, set up my two-piece, castleconnelsplice rod that I had spokeshaved myself, ran a silk line through the rings, knotted on a trace and a four-inch Blue Devon minnow, slung a fishing-bag on my shoulders, stuck a telescope gaff down the back of my neck, lit a pipe, and away with me for the river, bound for hell or glory: an honest angler for all the world to see, full of hope on a hopeless morning.

No one was about that early, but many of the chimneys sent up a curl of smoke, to show that the housewives were busy at the porridge pots. But though I saw no one, no doubt a man here and there had a peep at me through a window-pane, and wondered what Michael Danny was up to so early in the day, and what the Devil did he expect to catch, anyway?

Down the slope, near the village-end, I came to Dan Casson's house, a neat thatched cottage, blue-white with a few feet of green in front, and a clump of daffodowndillys yellow out of the grass. It was a good viewpoint for a peeping Tom, for it commanded a winding mile of the river up and down. There was a thick drift of peat smoke from the chimney to show that someone was up and the fire new-lit. So I leant over the wicket-gate and let a bawl out of me.

'Dan—Dan Casson, you—!' and the word I used in a lower voice I don't use often.

The house was silent. So I cleared my throat and tried again.

'Dan Casson, you hound! Show a leg!'

And there the door opened, and Katty, his wife, put out her red head. A gay and gallant devil she always was, tied to a stick-in-the-mud, but content with the tie for some reason I could never understand.

'Save us all, Uncle Mike!' says she. 'Is the house on fire?'

'It will be. Listen here to me! When your sluga-bed wakes up tell him Michael Danny is gone fishing, and that he'll fish the Ludin Pool and the Urdog Pool and the Corrig Pool, and, what's more, he'll land a fish, and Dan Casson can come and watch him do it. Tell him that, red-head! I'll be looking for him.'

She hesitated, and came out on the step, shoving her blouse inside her bellyband.

'I can't,' she said with some meaning.

'Why not, dammit?'

'Dan is not in,' she told me, her voice low.

'Ho-ho! is he on the river this early? Good enough! I'll be seeing him.' And I turned to go.

'Wait, Uncle Mike!' she called after me, and came down to the gate. I waited. She was barefoot at this hour, and she had shapely feet, like all my family.

She was my only niece, and we liked each other well, and it could be that she was not too happy about her husband's job. Anyway, she kept her eyes on her hands fumbling each other, and her voice was not much more than a whisper.

'Dan is not here at all, Uncle Mike.' That is what she told me.

'He'll not be far away, surely?'

'Fifty mile is far enough. Word came to him in the middle of the night by phone to the Guards Barracks that he's wanted in Limerick to-day for an urgent meeting with the Fishing Conservators.'

Outside the fishing-hotels, the only phone in the village was in the Civic Guard station, and the Guards, like kindly men, relayed any message that came through.

'Glory be!' said I. 'Dan is getting to be an important man.'

'He is not, then,' said she warmly. 'He has to answer a complaint some divil made against him.'

'I'm glad to hear it,' said I. 'He was always too good to be true.'

'Never, Dan Casson, you old divil!' she said, half-laughing and half mad. 'He was so wild that he hit the ceiling, and cycled six miles to Barnagh to catch the milk-train to Limerick, at the skreek o' dawn.'

Her voice went to a whisper' 'I wouldn't tell it to anyone but yourself, Uncle Mike.'

'And I'm as deaf as a post,' I said. 'If the worst comes to the worst he'll get the sack—and I hope he will. All right, my darlint! Give Dan my message when he comes back, and I'll go and catch my fish.'

'Catch it honest—if you are able,' said she, and one live eye seemed to hood itself at me as she turned away.

I had said that I would land a fish, but, to judge by the weather and the water, I might as well be fishing a rain-splash in a rut. It was a still, chill morning, with a clear sky and a ground frost, and the river was as low as ever I had seen it, even in the heat of July. And there was a sort of an oily sheen on the surface of the pools that, for some reason, is never or seldom broken by a rising fish.

I looked over the Ludin Pool, a narrow reach with a curve in it like my little finger, and I made three casts to sort of fulfil the prophecy. Then I went on up to the Urdog Pool, a wide, shortish pool like the flat of my thumb, and I made three casts there too. And again I went on, and round the corner to the Corrig Pool. The Corrig is a secluded pool, with high shelving banks of limestone, and shelving slabs of limestone under the surface, and some of it was ten foot deep even in that low water. In the Corrig Pool was the fish I wanted.

Look now! I had been watching that fish for days. So had every fisherman in The Village. So had Dan Casson. A cock fish, with an underjaw like the prow of a gan'lo,[1] a monster of a fish, the biggest fish ever

---

[1] A Kerry fishing-boat—gondola.

seen in the Ullachowen, bigger than any fish ever taken out of it, lord of the Corrig Pool. If it wouldn't scale thirty pounds, it would scale more.

It had a habit, two or three times a day, of butting slowly up into the throat of the pool and drifting back to the tail, flukes first, and then coming out of the water in a slanting drive and fall that sounded like a clap of thunder, and sent fat rings lap-lap under the overhang of the rocky banks. After that it would steer across to its favourite resting-place on a flat shelf three foot under water, its prow upstream, and holding its place against the drift with a lazy turn of its big flukes. It disdained any sort of honest lure under the sun, and we daren't use the other kind.

That was the fish I wanted. That was the fish we all wanted. That was the fish Dan Casson was watching like the apple of his eye.

And to make a long story short that was the fish I got.

Yes, sir! I got him. He gave me plenty of trouble, and I took a long time, jockeying him into position, throwing a lump of stone to stop him sulking in throat or tail, moving him patiently here and there, until finally I got him within reach of the gaff. And then I let him have it, and heaved him out with force enough to land me on the flat of my back. He was buck-humping on the slabs as I scrambled to my feet, and I quieted him with a kick on the poll. And after that I sat on my heels for to admire and for to see.

He was a grand fish, beyond any manner of doubt, not too lengthy, but with the girth and shoulders and sides of a fattening pig. And, though he had been some time in river water, his silver was barely tarnished, and there was no more than a faint pink tinge on sides and keel. The scales I had in the bag only pulled to thirty pounds, and when I set the hook of it in his beak and drew the thirty pounds his big tail was still on the rock. He was thirty-five pounds if an ounce. I could call it forty, but I won't, being a fair man.

I did no more fishing that day. I took my fish home, the tail of him projecting from the bag over the top of my head, and, as a middling modest angler, I did not parade him before envious eyes. I went the back way, but I took care to be seen by someone here and there, who did not pretend to see me slinking home, as it might be, with a salmon not legally mine. Then, if it came to the bit, every man, woman and child in The Village could swear that they had never seen Michael Danny and his big fish.

But still the word went out, and it went far and wide as I heard later: Michael Danny had caught the monster, and the weight of it, by degrees, went up to fifty pounds: but how had the devil caught it, and what was the new river warden doing about it, and where in hell was the new river warden, anyway? Katty Casson kept her mouth shut, and so did I.

Naturally, all the fishermen in The Village wanted to come and see my prize, but, according to our tradition, they had to behave with restraint and indifference. No one at all looked in on me till the lamp was lit that evening, and the first man that came was our young Schoolmaster, who had written 'The Chronicles of The Village' but daren't publish them in dread of twenty-seven actions for libel. He was no mean fisherman himself.

'Is it true, Michael Danny?' said he.

'What?' said I.

'That you caught, landed, and slew, one way or another, the father of all the fishes?'

'Look for yourself!' said I, careless kind of, turning a thumb towards the dresser, where I had laid the fish on a bed and under a cover of cabbage leaves, to keep it from going too dry. It filled the whole shelf.

The Schoolmaster stripped the leaves off, and looked, and stepped back, and looked again. He said nothing, but his whistle expressed all that it should. He examined the fish's mouth, and I knew he was looking for the hook-marks of the minnow. He found them. He looked at the gash of the gaff-stroke, and it was as it should be. He examined the fish's scales, and turned it over, and I knew he was looking for the scrape of a treble hook—what we call a stroke-haul. He didn't find it. Then he nodded at me.

'A first-class pass with honours!' he said. 'That beauty will stand inspection anywhere—as far as the Recording Angel, anyway.'

'And it will pass him as well,' I said.

'It might,' he agreed. 'He wouldn't know about the Game Laws.'

After that the lads started coming, and they came in their old numbers—the whole school of them. Maybe they knew that something was in the wind. I didn't— or, at least, I wasn't sure. The salmon was examined and finger-girthed and criticised and praised with makebelieve indifference; and there was side-talk I was not supposed to hear, though it was spoken for my ear, about Dan Casson and what was he doing at all to let Michael Danny get away with a bare-faced operation in broad daylight?

The news of the big fish had spread sure enough, for Detective Inspector Wren of the Guards drove up in his car to see for himself. He was as decent a spud of an Ulsterman as ever drew breath, and that's saying a good deal; a first-class angler himself, and many a good day—and night—we had together. All the same, I wasn't too pleased to see him, in the circumstances, but I had to play the cards as they lay. He bent under the lintel, and lifted his voice in the pawky Northern way.

'My name is Thomas, and I doubt everything. Michael Danny never caught any monster this weather?'

'Let your eyes belie you, Inspector,' said I, and pointed a finger.

He went across and looked, and after a while he spoke in a quieter voice.

'Rumour is a lying jade, but that is one real fish. My congratulations, Michael.' He looked at me in a funny way. 'He gave you some sport, old boy?'

'Sport and trouble in plenty, but I got him where I wanted in forty minutes.'

'On what?' said he, with a side-glance at the fish.

'On a four-inch Blue Devon,' I told him. 'See the mark of it there on his gob—'

And there an angry growl came from behind my back.

'To hell with your *Blue Devon*, Michael Danny! That fish was lifted on a gaff and nothing else, and I'll swear it to my dying day.'

I was not taken by surprise, for I had heard the down train whistle for Barnagh Tunnel half an hour before. I turned and faced Dan Casson. The time had come.

His wide mouth was twisting itself out of control, and his black brows were knotting and unknotting themselves. We stared at each other eye to eye, and the kitchen shut down to silence. Everyone there knew that the test was on between Dan Casson and me, but no one knew it better than myself. So I kept as cool as spring-water.

'You are welcome back, Dan, my poor fellow!' I greeted him. 'Where have you been the live-long day?'

If Dan Casson had kept his mouth shut then, he might have saved his thin skin. But he was so mad, and in such a hurry to accuse me, that he lost any discretion he ever had. His voice went up into a screech.

'Dam' well you know where I was, Michael Danny, after the dirty trick you played me.'

You could hear a pin drop in the silence all round us. The boys were beginning to see.

'How would I know where you were,' said I, 'and how could I play a trick on Dan Casson, the smartest river warden in all Ireland?'

'Ho—ho—ho!' There was that one bark of a laugh, and again the dead silence.

Dan, like a baited bull, shook his head, and faced the police-inspector. He had his voice in better control now.

'My enemies make a laugh of me, but I am asking you Inspector Wren, to witness what I have to say.'

'Go on, Casson!' said the Inspector in his quiet way.

'A telephone message came to me from Limerick late last night—or was it Limerick?'

'It was,' the Inspector told him. 'It is on record at the Garda Station.'

'Very well so! The message said I was to go up to Limerick to-day to talk with the Conservators about a complaint'—his voice lifted and shook—'a dasterly complaint that I was gaffing salmon on the sly and selling them to the hotels at the seaside.'

I lifted my hand and my voice.

'And did you, Dan?' said I.

'I wouldn't put it past him,' shouted young Eamon Broder.

'Dan, did you?' And Tom Roddy pointed a finger.

And for half-a-minute there was a chorus of: 'Did you, Dan? Dan, did you?'

Dan lifted his fists up in the air, and his face was awful to behold. The Inspector moved a hand for silence, and got it.

'Go on, Casson!' said he.

Dan's voice was desperate quiet, beyond and beyond all emotion.

'I went up to Limerick by the milk-train. There was no meeting of the Conservators. There was no complaint agin me. There was no telephone message from the head office. I was tricked away from home' —he pointed a finger at me— 'and while I was away that man there gaffed the fish I was watching for weeks. I accuse him.'

Every man there waited for me to answer that, and I did. Dan had his finger pointed at me like a dagger, and I pointed my finger back at Dan.

'You were fooled away to Limerick, Dan?'

'You know I was.'

I stabbed my finger at him. 'Do you know the day that's in it, Dan?'

'Wednesday—!'

'Wednesday the First Day of April, Dan! All Fools' Day!'

His mouth fell open, and his hand dropped.

'All Fools' Day, Dan Casson!' I drove it home. 'Someone made an April Fool of you all the way to Limerick, and as an April Fool you'll be known all your days.'

There was one united yell that nearly lifted the roof, and a gale of laughter, that is always cruel, and strangulated voices crying, 'April Fool! April Fool.' Inspector Wren turned his back.

Dan Casson stared at me, his mouth hanging open, and the poison working into him. I thought he was going to jump me, and I had a fist handy to spread him on the floor.

But he only made a hopeless motion with both hands, and a staggering rush for the door. I was sorry then, and often I have been sorry since; but, as I pointed out to you, something had to be done, and 'tis better be an April Fool once a year, than a dumb carcase forever.

There is no need to tell you more. If you want to know, Dan Casson sent in his resignation next day, and shortly after that went back to East Limerick, where he belonged. And life in The Village resumed its normal course.

The annoying thing to me is that no one will believe that I caught that big fish honestly. You don't believe it either. But, do you know, by dint of frequent narration, I am beginning to believe it myself.

THE HOPLOLOGIST

BROTHERS they were, the two of them. And what is more, they were twin brothers; but not similar twins, or identical twins, or whatever the term is. That is in outward appearance; and whether they were sib or not below the surface we shall be seeing if the Lord spares me the use of my tongue.

Larry, the elder by a split minute, was a big, lean, swank lad, sporting a curly wave of black hair, a face of dark comeliness, and a pair of black eyes with the devil behind them and they set on a shapely woman—or a shapelier bottle of Irish whiskey; and give him the bottle most times. He was good with his hands, and good at games; the best company in the world, drunk or sober, whether in a saloon bar or a lady's boudoir; a devil to tell a story on the far edge of decency, and with a mellow baritone voice to charm a bird off a bough. And, look, he had brains to burn, and could extract meat out of a textbook same as you'd extract a periwinkle out of its shell on the point of a pin.

Timothy—Timmy for short—the other twin, was small by comparison—under middle height, slim and neat in build, fair in the skin and fair in the hair, and grey eyes diffident when any woman at all turned head to look at him. As a student he was steady but slow, and in his leisure hours—not so many—he was given to day-dreaming and versification, save the mark, probably seeing himself a mile high and a mile wide playing the lute to his own song under his lady's window—or inside it.

There you have the two of them now, and do you see a shade of similarity in their make-up? You don't—not yet!

Their father was a fairly strong farmer away down on the Kerry border, and they were the youngest of seven or eleven brothers and sisters. So the only fortune they got was the sort of education that would fit them for the church or a stockbroker's office or the Civil Service. And the Civil Service it was.

At the age of eighteen, or it might be twenty, the two of them sat the entrance examination to a certain department that shall be nameless for the very good reason that one of them is in it yet, and you might easily put a finger on him. And, as luck would have it, they were successful the first time of asking. Big Larry, after a two months' intensive grind, took the first place in all Ireland; and Timmy, after years of plodding, took the nineteenth, which was not the last successful place, but the second last, and not so dusty either, considering that there were a hundred also-rans behind him.

In due course they were called up to Dublin and took their humble places in a big office among a score or two of their subhuman species—writing assistants clacking at typewriters, clericals drawing double lines, executives pretending to make decisions of nation-wide importance. They went into digs on a quiet street off the Circular Road, and in their own opinion they were on top of the world, the ball at their feet, the field open before them, and the goal of a Secretary-ship in the not-too-far distance.

They made progress, I can tell you that, and, for a beginning, you could not see Larry for dust, with Timmy lost in it far behind, but coming—coming in his own solid way. At the end of five or seven years Timmy had a desk of his own in the big office, and a fourth share of a lady typist; but by that time Larry had a room to himself, with a carpet on the floor, and a swivel-chair, and a typist and a couple of clericals to jump to his beck-and-call.

Old mother nature is not very original. She has not many patterns to work from, and she used one of them here. Listen, now! Timmy had a fourth share of a typist, as I said, and, in process of time and propinquity, he wanted more, and then more, for she fitted his dreams to a nicety; and fine dreams he had —his own fire corner and his slippers warming on the hob, a chess problem at hand, and his lady-of-the-house, the other side of the fire, deferring to the wisdom he was producing with such ease and felicitation. You know? Dreams like that, and growing in intimacy like the days lengthening.

Her name was Emer, and she had her share of good looks, with green eyes alive under copper hair; and, besides, she was gay and gallant, with a bit of pleasant devilment at heart; and she had a nice way of making pleasant play of Timmy's seriousness and diffidence. And, mind you, she was liking Timmy, and warming a corner of her heart for him, and warming it a bit more, and a bit more, until—

Ay, until! Until big Larry, the bad devil, set eyes on her, and approved of what he saw. And he saw, too, how things were with Timmy, and the road Timmy was going, and the end of it; and that end he did not approve at all. 'Powders o' war!' said he to himself. 'Before I know where I am that stick-in-the-mud twin of mine will be nobbled by the red-head, and that is a thing I can't afford at all. There's that three hundred pounds I need for the new car, and Timmy has it, as well I know, and no need for it. Steps will have to be taken.'

And steps were. By a bit of office manœuvring Larry shifted his own typist on to another colleague and got Emer promoted into her place. There he had her under his hand and eye, and loosed all his charm on her; and charm the devil had, the dark and vibrant charm that had helped to pitch Lucifer and his cohorts into the pit of hell.

To make a long story short, Emer fell for Larry good and hard, but not hard enough to suit him, for she was a girl of character and integrity, and the only invitation she would accept, and there were many, was an invitation to the marriage rails. This astounded Larry of the easy conquests, and nettled him too, and put him on his mettle, and made Emer all the more desirable, and finally blinded him into taking the plunge into matrimony. He even pretended to be philosophic about it. 'Ah well,' said he to himself, 'as long as the fox runs he gets caught at last; and maybe it is time for me to come to anchor in a port of my own choice— and, begobs, an anchor can always be slipped to suit the occasion; and haven't I Timmy always, the emasculated creature, to look after the house and a bill or two—and the wife as well, and he looking up to her as if she was a queen not to be touched by hands.'

So Larry and Emer were married. And Timmy, his face calm but desolate, was best man. And Timmy, under instructions, acquired a house for the young couple—a semi-detached villa out Sandymount way—and, what is more, he went to live with them. He did not want to live with them, desperately he did not want that; and Emer did not want it either, for she knew how Timmy felt, and was sorry for him—and a bit ashamed of herself. But Larry was his usual dominant self, and had his own way—as usual. 'Sure, Timmy boy,' said he, 'haven't we been together all our lives, sharing everything together, and why should we change now?' He slapped Timmy on the back. 'Begod, sir, there is nothing I would not share with you—nothing at all, and that's flat.' And he winked lasciviously. Timmy had an urge to belt him across the dirty mouth, but the courage failed him.

This is not Larry's story. It is Timmy's story, and I am getting to it with might and main. But, first, I have to get Larry off the stage, and keep him off it until his last dramatic entry.

Emer had three children—two sons and a daughter—in ten years. And in the same ten years her husband, big Larry, went all to hell—eternal hell not yet.

He was a brilliant devil, and his superiors were slow in finding out his shortcomings, but they got round to them in time. Larry was a hard drinker on the road to dipsomania; he was a gambler prepared to cheat; he was a philanderer without morals. He made reckless mistakes that even his ability could not cover; his files piled up on him; he evaded responsibility by taking sick-leave and more sick-leave, until an official inquiry found him, not in a sick-bed, but at Leopards-town Races with a lady of some virtue.

He was demoted from his grade, pulled himself together temporarily, was promoted again, and again lapsed; and at the end of ten years he was at last suspended, and, a month later ignominiously dismissed without a hope of reinstatement.

Yes, sir, at the age of thirty-five Larry was finished forever and a day—as a careerist. But that did not worry Larry, not any more. His disgrace slipped off him like water off a duck's back, for he was become a depraved and evil man, and morale no longer had any meaning for him—if it ever had. He lived unashamedly and shamelessly, smugly and boastingly, like—like a deposed monarch—on his brother and on his own wife.

There was nothing the two could do about it. Indeed, there was nothing they wanted to do, for, if the truth must be told, the sort of equilibrium that was achieved at the Sandmount villa suited Timmy and Emer well enough. The house was by no means un-happy, and don't think it was—apart from a natural frustration.

Big Larry was seldom at home, maybe twice in a month to replenish the exchequer, a thing Timmy was ever ready to do to be rid of him. And once he was three months away, in Mountjoy Jail, for driving off and wrecking another man's car. And it is more than probable that some dirty money stuck in his fingers in proceedings that shall be nameless.

Timmy, who had, in fact, taken charge of household affairs from the very beginning, merely went on with the job. He was fond of Emer in his own steadfast way, and he grew fond of Emer's children. He played about with them, helped them with their lessons in due time, took them to the zoo on a frequent Sunday in summer, took their mother to the pictures or a play at the Abbey once a week, and on an occasion stood her a slap-up dinner in Jammet's Restaurant. Begod, sir, it looked like an ordinary, unromantic married establishment in suburbia, with husband and wife living amicably together, and the black sheep of the family turning up occasionally with a hard-luck story.

No doubt certain scandalous tongues went awagging, but without reason, as far as I know. And sometimes Larry, in the lachrymose stage of intoxication, would weep over his uncalled-for misfortunes, and deplore himself for a cuckold, and promise all the devils in hell that he would take a day off, some time, to disrupt, dismember, and disembowel his traitor twin. As if Larry would ever kill his goose!

As regards Emer, I don't know, not being acquainted with the inner workings of the female species. One thing certain, she no longer loved her husband—and hadn't for ten years. Maybe for some purpose of her own she maintained her looks and desirability, and did not go slattern like many a wastrel's wife; and, anyway, it was good to have Timmy attached to the house, if not to her apron-strings—that is so long as he remained satisfied with the two little hobbies he pursued. I will come to them later.

This is Timmy's story, and we are at it.

His worth in his department was slowly recognised,

and then recognised wholeheartedly. From nine to five, five days a week, he was the perfect administrator —exploring every avenue, reaching a conclusion slowly but not leisurely, altering a decision like a mountain in travail and then bringing forth the mouse like a clap o' thunder. He could start a verbiage beginning, 'adverting to,' and finish it in the middle of next week. He could devise, create, and promulgate an official form to be signed three times in triplicate, with a questionnaire that no taxpayer could fill in short of one brainstorm—maybe two. He could keep a file alive, or at least moribund, longer than any other official anywhere; and there was one famous file, pride of the service, that took four messengers and a wheelbarrow to get borne into the Presence on ceremonial occasions. And, so and inevitably, Timmy went on and on, and up and up—from Junior to Higher Executive, to Assistant Principal, to Principal, with an Assistant Secretaryship within his grasp, and a Secretaryship in the offing.

Outside office hours, day in day out, year after year, you would take him for a staid and law-abiding denizen of one of the deserts of suburbia, and be ready to bet your immortal soul on it. But you wouldn't be too sure if you knew the two little hobbies he was given over to. Ay, two hobbies, but you might call one of them a vice.

That doubtful hobby—or vice—was drink. D-R-I-N-K! And the king of all drinks for male man —ten-year-old Irish whiskey. Aha, you will say, the twin in him is showing forth at last? Or frustration? Maybe so. But where one twin was a profligate dipsomaniac, the other was a continent imbiber, regulating his drink as he regulated his work. I don't mean that Timmy regaled himself daily with one or two or three or four balls o' malt. No man who does that only can call himself a drinking man. No, sir, this is what Timmy did.

Once a month, no more and no less, on a certain Saturday evening after tea, Timmy depraved his neat little body by investing it in the shabbiest, shapelessest old suit o' tweeds ever handed down from a second-hand shelf; twisted a blue bird's-eye muffler round his collarless neck; stuck a dirty-shiny peaked stevedore cap over one eye; and disappeared from respectable purlieus for thirty hours.

Where did he go? I'll tell you that too. He went into town, he crossed the Liffey, he went down by the Quays, he took two turns to the left and one to the right, and slipped in by the lounge-door of a certain hotel and hostelry that shall be nameless for reasons not stated. That is the place where Timmy went.

Maybe it was a fourth-rate hotel; maybe it was a low pub; but it was not a mean one. Good order was kept, as gentlemen to gentlemen and the liquor was the best, and the best only; no woman, virtuous or spendthrift, was allowed inside the door of bar or lounge; men only, and not every man either, had a right to put a foot on the brass rod or wallop an emphatic fist on a scarred table-top—seaworthy men, wandering troubadours suffering the usual eclipse, writing Johnnies on the make, seekers of oblivion on the dodge from Mrs Grundy, and those wonderful working-men of Dublin who could out-talk Villon and down pints of Guinness to the confoundment of biologists who hold that the capacity of the human stomach is only a quart-and-a-half. One of them, one time, on a bet, drank five pints in five minutes, a thing contrary to nature. 'You did it, Jerry,' says his backer, 'but it was a dam' close thing.' 'It was so,' agreed Jerry through the high tide in his thrapple, 'but I knew I could do it. Sure, I tried it up at the Red Cow before coming along here.' Yes, sir!

Timmy's practice never varied. He would slip in quietly looking at no one, take the same chair in the same quiet corner fenced in by a small table, and lift one finger. And customers, here and there, would nod and wink and prepare for eventualities.

And to the lift of Timmy's finger a barman would bring across a ball o' malt—a glass of ten-year-old Irish, pale-straw in colour; and Timmy, slowly and meticulously, would add a modicum of ten drops of water, and toss the mixture straight down on the pit of his stomach; and again lift one finger. He would do the same thing with the second ball o' malt, and the identical same thing with the third one. But not with the fourth—never with the fourth.

He would look at the fourth on the table-top, and smile at it in a friendly fashion, and sit up as if waking out of a day-dream. And after a while he'd rise slowly to his feet, pick up his glass, move with slow dignity to the long bar where a place was waiting for him, put a foot on the brass rod and an elbow on the zinc, clear his throat portentously, and in a voice resonant as a clarion enunciate something like this: 'Ned Keogh yonder, usually accurate, was holding forth last month that the mongoose fighting the king-cobra owes its safety entirely to its activity. That is not so, Edward my friend. Mongooses—not mongeese you will note, and you will also note that the plural of a certain Amerindian tribe is not Blackfeet but Blackfoot— mongooses in the death-struggle with their inveterate enemy are frequently wounded, but possess a large degree of immunity to the deadly venom. I recall an incident that I personally observed at Ahmednuggur in the Province of Bombay . . .'

Ay, begad! And the furthest he ever was outside Ireland was the Kish Light off Dublin Bay—in a rowboat. You need not believe me, but I'm telling you—when Timmy got to his fourth drink he began to be the grandest company within the four seas of Erin, and without a restraining inhibition in his whole small carcass.

He had an extraordinary volume of tone, and could shake the cobwebs off the ceiling with ballads like *Bold Phelim Brady* and the *Battle of Keimeneigh*; he would stand a drink here and take a drink there, and propose a toast with humour and felicitation; he would enter into a learned discussion on any subject under the sun, listening to another man's points with impatient courtesy and producing his own theses with some outrageous incidents that had befallen him in foreign parts—the headwaters of the Nile, the Cordilleras of Patagonia, or any dam' place so long as it was far enough off. And, do you know, his incidents were related with such verisimilitude of time and place and climate and flora and fauna that you could not help

believing him—at the time. Ay, faith, the finest
company in all Dublin while the bout lasted. . . . But
let a veil be drawn. . . .

Thirty hours was his dead limit. At midnight on
Sunday he slipped away like the Arab of old, still biled
as an owl but steady as a rock on his feet; took the
three turns on to the Quays wide and easy; crossed the
Liffey by the Butt Bridge; perambulated the three
miles out to Sandymount; and so to bed.

And on Monday morning he shaved and bathed,
clothed himself in official buckram, and sedately
proceeded to his devastating pursuit of useless ratiocina-
tion for another month.

But, take note of this, if you have not noted it
already—from the time that he had reached his fourth
drink on Saturday evening until he waked up on
Monday morning he suffered a complete blackout,
a blankness like a wall where no faintest shadow of
memory was ever cast. That is not unusual with
hard drinkers. And sometimes he used to wonder how
many men had quailed before him, and maidens
wilted in the glance of his eye. Let it be.

Timmy's other little proclivity was a real hobby.
He was a hoplologist. Hoplology! That shook you,
my good sir. Why, there is a society, with world-wide
correspondents, called The Right Worshipful Company of Hoplologists. The word hoplologist is from
the Greek, of course, and it means a collector of
weapons—not firearms, but swords and similar instru-
ments of evil: every class of weapon to slit a throat,
cleave a head, or pierce a wame. And Timmy was a
hoplologist. The twin showing, you will say again.

The brute in one brother subdued to a mere collector of weapons of destruction in the other! It might be.

Up in the double-attic of the house at Sandymount, with a Yale lock on the door, so that the young ones would not commit hara-kiri, Timmy had a sample of every blame weapon you could put a name to, and some you never heard of—broadsword, claymore, sabre, cutlass, rapier, small-sword, falchion, scimitar, yataghan, talwar, kukri, kris, sumarai, halberd, battle-axe, assegai, and I don't know how many more, arranged in patterns on the wall, catalogued and cross-indexed in Civil Service fashion, and with a history attached, where possible.

He had a rust-eaten iron sword that Sigurd of Caithness bore at the battle of Clontarf in 1014 before Murrough slew him; he had a Dervish spear that had killed a 21st Lancer in the gorge at Omdurman, and had gone within an ace—ochone, the day!—of killing Winston Churchill, who was a war correspondent at the time; he had an enormous straight French cuirassier sword still embedded in a portion of the skull it had cloven at Waterloo; he had an Andrea Ferrara that had flashed down the line at Fontenoy and fallen from the dead hand of a clansman on Culloden Moor; he had—I don't know all he had, but they were a bloodthirsty collection sure enough; and Timmy used to handle and gloat over them in bloodthirsty daydreams.

There was, however, one notorious weapon that he had not got, and that he, or any hoplologist the world over, would give half his collection to possess. That was one of the Chinese Emperor's personal swords—

the Doom Sword—the Blade of a Thousand Cuts— the sword that was never drawn except to destroy evil.

There is mention of thirteen of these all down history and tradition. Four of them have never been identified; eight of them are placed here and there in a museum or private collection; the thirteenth—the sword of Yung Lo, the son of Chu Yuan-Chang of the Ming Dynasty—was looted from a palace in Peking that time Chinese Gordon set out to show the Oriental the benefits of opium and Western civilisation.

Every hoplologist is interested in that looted sword and its whereabouts. Timmy's notion was as good as the rest: the sword was swiped by a British soldier who did not know its value, and, ultimately, it might be found hanging about in some old manor-house of military tradition anywhere in England, Scotland, Wales, or Ireland—and Ireland for choice, for sure an Irish soldier would loot the cross off an ass's back in foreign parts. That is why Timmy took a day off to visit every auction of old houses and old furnishings within easy reach of Dublin. He picked up a few good blades too, but not the blade of all blades. Until!

Ay, until! And now we are coming to the crux. As you know, swords and other snickersnees have been slowly but surely going out of fashion since the invention of villainous saltpetre, until now, in the atom age, they can be regarded as obsolete. In any auction-room in Dublin you can acquire a bundle of sabres for a pound note; and in any crumbling manor-house down the country you'll find half a dozen from basement to attic, and sometimes you'll find a broken one used as a poker.

Well, sir, on a certain Wednesday, Timmy caught a bus at O'Connell Bridge that took him down to view an old house and furniture up for auction on the Wexford border. The forefathers of that old house had been with Cromwell at Clonmel, and William at Steenkirk, and Marlborough at Malplaquet—and finally, with Chinese Gordon in the Opium Wars. And, of course, there was a bundle of old weapons tied with a piece of rope.

You know well what happened. Dambut, the Sword of Doom was in that careless bundle of old iron! The bundle was propped in a corner of the big hall amongst a lot of old junk. At the back of the bundle a tall hilt stood up from the other hilts—a two-handed hilt without a guard, and it was that hilt without a guard that gave Timmy his first flaming hint of the prize. He couldn't believe his eyes—or could he? Looking round to see that no one was observing him, he shuffled forward amongst the bric-à-brac, and turned the bundle of blades round to get a better view. Was it too good to be true? But true it was, and in two minutes Timmy made sure of the truth, his heart beating hard and high.

He knew all there was to be known about Yung Lo's sword—the guardless hilt, with the two little ivory household gods of the Emperor caught under the gilt wrapping, the Emperor's sign-writing bitten deep on the back of the blade just below the hilt, the shallow channel at each side of the heavy back, the half-inch of curvature on the lower half of the blade, the square-cut tip: they were all there. The sheath of plain yak-mak wood had perished near the tip and showed the blunt end. The blade was something under four feet in length, as it should be.

Carefully Timmy drew eighteen inches of the blade from its sheath and examined the condition of the metal. It had an edge knife-keen, and the blue-silver sheen of it showed scarcely a trace of tarnish, for the Emperor's swordsmith already knew something of oxidisation. Timmy gave the hilt a little jerk, and listened for a dulled tinkle. He heard it. That was the final proof, for the tinkle came from a sealed, longitudinal chamber in the back of the blade below the point of balance, where steel pellets ran free in a ball-race, so as to add power to the slash. Surely the sword was the missing Doom Sword.

That auction lasted the best part of four days, and, as usual, the junk was kept for the final day, and the bundle of swords was the final item put up for sale. The auctioneer would have put up the bundle at any time if Timmy had approached him, but Timmy did not, for he was afraid of attracting attention to his find. So he took four days' private leave and spent three-an-a-half of them on the point of a sword as it were, and his eyes everywhere on the lookout for a rival.

About noon on Saturday the auctioneer made a washing motion with his hands, and sighed with satisfaction. Devil the thing he knew about hoplology, but he would be facetious after the manner of his tribe. 'The final item, ladies and gents, and someone is due for a bargain.' His voice rang clear but hoarse, and no wonder. 'Here now is a historic set of bone-breakers—the sword of Brian Boru, who knows, or the slasher of our noble Sarsfield, or Wolfe Tone's stainless blade! Who'll bid me twenty pounds the lot?'

Some dealer chuckled derisively, and that was all.

'Come on! I'm not waiting. Start the ball rolling with fifteen quid? Ten? Five, then? No!' He smashed his mallet against his palm. 'Very well, then! I'll not waste any more time. Who'll bid me a pound?'

Timmy lifted a quiet forefinger.

'A pound!' The auctioneer smashed down his mallet. 'A bargain I said, and a bargain it is. They are yours for a pound. Take them away, sir—and kill your man with any of them.'

Ay, that is what he said, the joker—'*Kill your man with any of them.*'

Timmy paid his pound, and wrestled the bundle of swords under an oxter. They weighed like the very devil too, but the bus-stop was at the lodge gates only a hundred yards away. However, before he got there he came on a thick clump of shrubbery on the edge of the drive. Without hesitation he dodged round to the back of it, extracted his royal sword carefully, and carelessly toed its humble companions under the overhang of a bush. Mind you, there was a piece or two fit for a place in his collection, but he had got his great prize, and to hell with Brian Boru—the Lord forgive him! Then he fitted his Sword of Doom under the wing of his overcoat, with the long hilt standing up by his ear, and away with him back to Dublin, exultation bubbling in him.

It was six o'clock on a rainy October evening when he got there, but the high spirit in him did not mind the rain. The occasion surely called for a bit of a celebration, and for a start he treated himself to a slap-up meal in Jammet's—milk-fed chicken and Limerick ham, washed down by a tall bottle of Liebfraumilch 1934, a good year and a heady wine. And, like a ceremonial mace, his royal sword stretched on the table before him where no one might approach it with nefarious intent.

At first he had intended to ring up Emer to join him; and then he decided not to; and after a while he was glad he hadn't. And I'll tell you why.

It had been his intention, also, to go straight home after his meal, and bestow his precious sword in a safe place. But, as I said, Liebfraumilch is a heady wine, and already the revived little maggots of desire were wriggling in Timmy's brain and spinal column. And as is the way with men in the early stages of thirst he made excuses to himself. 'It is not my usual Saturday night, I know, and I am not attired for a descent amongst the proletariat; but all the same and nevertheless I would like the boys to see and admire my find and appreciate the great display of judgment that led me to it. And besides, not being my usual night, there is no danger, and I'll stay only one hour—one solitary hour and no more. Fair enough!'

So he went down to the washroom in Jammet's, removed his gent's collar and subdued tie, twisted a silk handkerchief loosely about his neck, knocked a dent in his respectable bowler-hat—and hied himself down by the Quays, his sword under coat and the hilt by his cheek. And begod, sir, already the little ivory gods under the lacing were beginning to whisper—queer, guttural little mutterings right into the drum of his ear.

Timmy took his three turns as usual, slipped through a lounge-door, and took his seat in his usual quiet corner. He laid his sword on the scarred board, and lifted one finger; and addicts winked and smiled, and prepared themselves for eventualities as usual.

Timmy did not reach his fourth ball o' malt that night. At the third he rose majestically to his feet, reached for the two-handed hilt, and cleared his throat portentously. The rich voice resounded. 'Gentlemen, behold the Doom Sword of Yung Lo, son of Chu Yuan-Chang, Emperor of the Ming Dynasty! Let me demonstrate.'

The great sword came swooping out of its broken sheath, crying as it came, and every man there got out from under. But let the veil be drawn. . . . One thing is certain—that night will not be soon forgotten in that low pub. By a miracle no blood was shed. There was harangue that went back and fore over ten centuries; there were recountings of strange and bloody incidents; and there were demonstrations to the risk of life and limb. The only neck that suffered was the neck of a Gold Label whiskey-bottle, and that went clean as a whistle through a mirror—at a cost to Timmy of thirty bob. A pewter pint-pot was sheared in half, same as you'd flick a thistle—that cost Timmy half-a-guinea. Bedad, sir, it was an ignoble perfor-·mance for a sword that had never been wielded but for the extirpation of evil, though I suppose a temperance advocate would call a bottle of whiskey and a pint-pot things of evil. But we have drawn the veil. . . .

The one pledged hour went by, and ten more with it. Indeed, the usual time went by, and at midnight on Sunday Timmy slipped away as usual, still biled as an owl, but as steady as an archbishop on his feet. No one would even venture to guess that he was as full as a tick. The rain was coming down heavens hard, and Timmy pulled his coat-collar about his ears, snuggled his cheek against the sword hilt, and took his three turns wide and easy. And again he heard little guttural murmurings in his ear.

You will not believe this. It might only be the drink talking in Timmy, but, as sure as death, the mutterings of the idol-gods were no longer indistinct; he could pick out words and phrases. '*Chang in one blow—Kuo-Sing, and a thousand cuts—still I thirst—all knots I cut—give me air and a neck of evil—air and a neck of evil.*' Over and over again. And it might be possible, if only dimly, that there came to Timmy the thought of a neck of evil. . . .

He came round by the long façade of the Custom House, where the tall lamps glistened on the pavements and glistered on the roily waters of the turbid and turgid Liffey. One of Guinness's steamboats, piled high with porter barrels, was moored close to the quay-wall, ready to go out with the morning tide. Timmy slanted across for Butt Bridge, keeping an unsafe distance from the edge of the quay. More than one man and a car or two have gone over that unguarded edge. The rain was still pouring, and no one, not even a cat, moved on the glistening asphalt.

Wrong! Two men moved. Timmy was one, and another man moved also. For as Timmy faced towards

48

a corner of the parapet another man came round it from the bridge. And that man was his twin brother, Larry.

What do you think of that? Larry coming out of a drunken spree? Larry like a hyæna, thirst ravening in him? Larry proceeding to one of his evil haunts? Larry moving as his fate willed him? Whatever it was, his footsteps had led him to this very spot face to face with his brother. And the devil was not far away.

Larry was bareheaded, and his black hair gleamed wetly under the lamps. However drink had besotted his mind, it had never coarsened his body. He was a lean limb of Satan, tall and upright, with gleaming black eyes, strong bosses of cheekbones above hollowed cheeks, and a strangely austere mouth—a distinguished-looking devil, as many devils are.

The two brothers, the big and the little, stopped and faced each other, and there was a hush of waiting all round them. The only sounds were the quiet sough of the falling rain, and a thin, cold tinkle of raindrops from the railway-bridge high overhead. And in that waiting hush Timmy again heard an urgent whisper in his ear. '*The evil neck only! Give me the air.*' That was the whisper.

Then Larry spoke, throwing up his hands in pleased surprise, and there was pleasure and surprise in his voice too. 'Well, oh well! My lucky night, and no doubt about it. Brother Tim on the loose, and myself in need of him!'

Ay, his lucky night! Timmy said nothing, for he was trying to draw his mind away from the alluring whisper in his ear: '*For the neck of evil I take the air.*'

'Sure, I ought to have known you were my twin under the skin,' said Larry. 'Man dear, have you anything good in your mind?'

'Good or evil, I do not know,' said Timmy deeply.

'A matter of outlook, the same good or evil,' said Larry agreeably, and his hand moved invitingly. 'There's a place I know not far from here, and you can make your own choice. Come along with me, you gay devil!'

'I will not come with you.' Timmy's voice was strong and definite, and then low and urgent. 'Go your own road, you blind fool—and go now.'

'Aha! You're on a trail of your own, are you? Very well so!'. Larry was still agreeable, but now came promptly to his own need, one hand out confidently. 'Would you have the loan of a fiver for me, Timmy boy?'

'I have not,' said Timmy, shaking his head against the insidious murmur that would not be silent.

'Murder alive!' cried Larry. 'But surely you'll have a quid or two to help me over the night?'

'I have no money on me,' said Timmy, and that was true. And some small, sane inner self was crying desperately: 'Oh God, if I only had a pound for him he would go away!'

'You're a bloody liar!' said Larry warmly. 'You were never short of a fiver in all your born days.'

'To-night I am,' said Timmy, and his voice lifted. 'Get out of my road!' Quickly he took two paces aside, but, alas, Larry was just as quick; and again the two brothers faced each other, almost breast to breast.

Timmy drew in his breath hissingly, and his hands came up towards the long hilt. But at the last moment sanity flashed again; his hands dropped, and he took two paces backwards. Behind him was the Liffey, and the edge of the quay was not three yards away.

Larry thrust his head forward, and put his hands on his hips. Here was threat of rebellion. Poor spineless Timmy! All the times he had threatened revolt, and all the times he had caved in—as he would cave in now. 'You haven't drink taken, Timeen?' he inquired half-mockingly.

'Buckets,' said Timmy. And buckets was right.

Larry laughed unbelievingly. He had never seen Timmy under the influence—in that queer, insanely sober state beyond the far edge of mere drunkenness. 'Wherever you got the courage,' he said, 'you will not deny your brother for the first time in your life.'

'Ten years ago I should have denied you,' said Timmy. And in a flash he realised what a desolation those ten years had been, a desolation where two frustrated lives had moved forlornly on broken wings, and where he himself had been driven to bouts of drinking for the surcease of misery.

'Is he going to be troublesome? I don't want to manhandle the little tomcat,' said Larry to himself. He took a quick glance up and down the Quays to see if the coast was clear, and it was. Unluckily for someone the coast was clear. Then he turned to Timmy and took a stride forward.

'Take one other step,' said Timmy warningly. He braced his legs, and his hands came up chin high. And the whisper in his ear: '*The air now—now—now!*'

'You and your foolish old gut-sticker!' sneered Larry, anger rising in him. 'Very well then! You go your way, and I go mine, a fiver in my pocket.' His voice snarled. 'Out with it!'

'Go your own road, you doomed fool!' said Timmy throatily.

And then a flame of insane rage leaped in Larry, as it will leap in a man long soaked in alcohol. His hands and his voice lifted, and the power of words came to him. 'You ungrateful pup-dog, that I cherished in my bosom all your useless days! You destroyer of house and home, that set me wandering the streets, a damn'd soul! You hanger-on to the apron-strings of another man's wife! You twin brother to a cuckold! Do you know what I am going to do to you now? Shake the last farthing out of you, and pitch your miserable carcase into the Liffey tide.'

'You foul-mouthed liar—' That is all that Timmy had time to say, for Larry launched forward, his hands out to clutch and wrench.

But Timmy was not there. Timmy side-stepped, lithe as an eel, and Larry stopped himself a stride from the edge of the quay, unbalanced for a moment, head and hands thrown forward.

Something flashed in the air; something gave an exultant double-cry; something, of its own volition, swooped and checked and swooped on. The force of that terrific swoop whirled Timmy round, and round again. He staggered, balanced precariously, and steadied himself on the very edge of the quay. He was looking down into the water. The water flowed sternly, turbidly, and heaved itself sullenly against

the stern of the steamer moored against the quay-wall.
And the only thing that moved was the water.

Timmy straightened up and turned round. He
was alone. Up and down the wide quay nothing
moved. 'My God, what mad vision was that?' he
cried.

On Monday morning Timmy awoke out of a dream-
less sleep, and, as usual, his mind was a blank wall
where no faintest shadow was cast of anything that had
befallen since this third whiskey on Saturday; nor,
indeed, did any weight of gloom press on him from the
unconscious.

But he remembered his Sword of Doom all right.
There it was, laid carefully along the top of his dressing-
table. He got out of bed and examined it with growing
satisfaction. The veritable article, as he could prove
to any envious hoplologist who dared to give challenge.

The hilt and the devilish little gods were still damp
from the night's rain; so was the broken sheath; so
was the blade when he drew it; and one faint, pinkish-
orange stain was drying in one of the groves. Timmy
did not even speculate as to what that stain might be.
He went to the bathroom, cleaned and polished the
sword, and hung it in the hot-press to dry thoroughly.

Thereafter he shaved and bathed, attired himself
in official buckram, ate a hearty breakfast, told Emer
of his find, glanced at the morning paper, and proceeded decorously to his devastating, many-branched,
but fruitless labours.

Listen now! You remember that Guinness boat by
the quay-wall? It cast off that morning to take Dublin
stout to thirsty Anglo-Saxons. The propeller-blades

threshed for two seconds, checked and stuck, and stayed stuck. Within an hour a diver discovered the gruesome cause of the stoppage. Within another hour the poor mangled remains were on the quay-wall. The threshing scoop of a propeller-blade was not merciful to frail humanity. An arm was torn away, so was a foot. *The head was also missing.*

A nameless body? No. A few sodden papers and an envelope or two gave name and address. And so, early that afternoon, Emer and Timmy identified the remains. That was not so difficult. There was a broken finger badly set, and there was a characteristic mole below the left shoulder-blade. Timmy, the twin, had a similar mole in the same place. And Timmy, the twin, had no inkling as to how his twin had died.

He had no inkling then. And he has no inkling now. For he has not taken a single ball o' malt since that fateful week-end. He no longer feels the craving for one. Why should he? He no longer suffers the frustation that drove him to whiskey for surcease.

Yes. Emer married him within the year, and he has a son of his own now.

But if ever he down four balls o' malt one on top of the other . . . I wonder!

TAKE YOUR CHOICE

ONCE upon a time—that is how all proper stories begin—once upon a time there was a young man, and the name of that young man was Sean, and he had a Fairy-Godmother. And she had a gift up her sleeve for him—or a rod in pickle, as the case might be, for with a Fairy-Godmother a gift-horse should always be looked in the mouth.

When Sean came of age his Fairy-Godmother paid him her final visit, and made speech as follows:

'Sean, my son, I have two gifts for the giving, and one of them is for you, and yours the choice.'

'I'll have the two,' said Sean promptly.

'Then there would be no problem, little rogue. No, no, one only! Listen now! One gift is a lady, young and fair and chaste, ready for love and eager for happiness. She has no dowry, but she has a woman's head and a woman's ambition, and she might lead you far. The other gift is twenty thousand pounds, and it is not fairy-gold. The choice is yours, and take your time to make it.'

A maiden fair and chaste and ready for love is all very well in her way, but those were the days when twenty thousand pounds meant twenty thousand golden sovereigns. Any young man in his senses would choose the twenty thousand, and acquire the maiden as easy as a cat lapping cream.

But Sean was young and foolish and romantic; and worldly ambition had not yet been stirred in him. He was all for love, and to the devil with filthy lucre! He chose the lady, young and fair and chaste, and his Fairy-Godmother smiled behind her hand.

In due course Sean met the young lady, and found her to his liking; and in due course they were joined in wedlock. They faced life debonairly, young enough still not to speculate on what an arid thing, what a sheltering thing, what an absorbing thing life in double harness can be. All that they knew was that they were to live happy ever afterwards, and possibly for a long time they did in a same, sane, steady, stable way.

The wife had ambition, no doubt of it, and a woman's head to plan for it, but her ambition was not unreasonable: a home to be proud of, and life in polite society. One cannot say that Sean was amenable, but he was pliable, and more than that a wife does not need. Within a year he was in the hollow of her hands without knowing it, for that is the way husbands have to be held lest they recognise themselves as tame mice.

She got Sean interested in business—and it does not matter what the business—and gradually BUSINESS became for him the most important thing in life. The sun rose in the morning to warn him that nine o'clock was approaching and his office waiting. The sun went down the sky to apprise him that he had an hour or two of lesiure to fit himself for another strenuous day.

He was elected Director of his Company and finally Chairman; he became a member of the Chamber of Commerce; and on one great occasion he was one of a Commission appointed to advise, direct, admonish, and reprimand the Minister for Industry and Commerce.

Sean safely balanced in a business niche, his wife set out to mould him to the life she had chosen. And Sean was as pliable as ever.

He built himself—he was sure it was himself—a detailed, semi-bungalow-type house in an exclusive suburb. He employed a gardener three days a week to curry-comb a curtilage of three roods. He went to business in a long-tailed American car, and presented his wife with a baby-eight to play with. After five years on a waiting-list he was elected member of a select nine-hole golf course, and in another five years won a monthly medal from a handicap of twenty-two.

He was a member of a commercial club in town, and played bridge there two nights a week; and, in a daring mood, sometimes took a hand at poker, sixpence calling a shilling. And on a rare festive occasion he embarked on a bit of a spree and went home in the dawn with one, or maybe three, over the eight under his belt.

Accompanied or led by his wife, he took three weeks' holiday most years, and was known to go as far afield as Paris or Lourdes, or even Cannes. He went to a race meeting once a month in summer and fall, and though he was never a footballer he was one of the privileged many to get a brace of admission tickets to Rugby internationals.

His wife took him to dances three times in the season, and permitted him to flirt innocuously with other men's wives; and, indeed, she was not above a nocuous bit of flirtation herself. She was a leading member of her suburban society, threw a cocktail party about Christmas time, gave a dinner after Lent, and ran a bridge school of twelve matrons where the game was only second in importance to the scandal that is usually talked at such gatherings.

There were three children of the marriage, as might be expected in a Christian community: two sons and a daughter. One son, who was neither clever nor able, was apprenticed to a stockbroker; the other son, who was clever but not able, took to party politics; but sure, a black sheep is found in most families. The daughter married a wholesale draper.

There is no need to go on detailing the life of suburbia. It sets no river on fire, but it is sane, sound, and stolidly successful. Sean lived it for forty years without one twinge of regret or one spark of imagination.

And then, at the age of sixty-plus—and he was still a hale and lively man—he had a terrible vision one night after three drinks too many. Possibly his Fairy-Godmother, in remote control, thought it time to take her rod out of pickle.

Sean dreamt that instead of the fair damosel he had chosen the twenty thousand sovereigns, and the dream went on from there to show him the life that he might have led. It was a thoroughly cautionary experience, even in a dream.

In that dream Sean simply went to the devil. Business? With twenty thousand sovereigns in hand business was only a negation of life. Marriage? Well yes! A more-than-mature woman took his fancy, and he married her, and she walked out on him for a worse man in less than a year, and he was glad to see her go. Drink? He drank when he had a mind to, and he generally had.

He gambled, and had gambler's luck, which is bad two times out of three. He bred a brace of tracking greyhounds and lost several shirts on them. He bought a middling-good racehorse, and, as all sportsmen know, a middling-good racehorse is the very worst horse to own. He hired himself a half-bred Irish hunter and went out with the harriers, but gave that up after breaking his collar-bone twice. . . . And he saw life, but how he saw it and where is another regrettable matter. . . .

But why go on? To make a long story short, Sean, in his dream, was as broke as bread in eight lively years. He hadn't a bean, but that never worried Sean. He just made a brushing motion with his hands and said:

'That is that! Now I'll see life where it is lived with nothing to cushion it.'

So on his own two feet he went out into the world, by highways and byways, path and track, mountain and moor, and lived as men of the road lived: often cold, often hungry, often too replete, but never weary to despair, never lonesome to regret, always interested and forever wondering. . . .

And in due course he joined fortune with a tinker-woman, and the two lived gloriously, riotously un-happily happy for many fast-moving years. And on a proper occasion Sean knew the thrill of tanning a woman's hide, and there is no thrill higher. . . .

In one fine culminating row the tinker-woman got in the last word with the lid of an iron skillet, and the shock woke Sean up to find himself fallen out of bed in his own chaste suburban bedroom.

He did not know where he was for all of a minute, and then, still sitting in the dark, he said a strange thing:

'Bedam! I am dreaming now. That was the real thing.'

But he was not dreaming, as he found out when he bumped his nose on his own bedpost. He did not dream any more that night, for he could not sleep another wink because of the queer thoughts running in his mind.

He roused himself with the birds in the dawn, and it was the dawn of a spring morning. The daze of that vivid dream was still on him, and he lay on his back wondering what life was at all, and what life should be on a spring morning. The answer came to him after a while, and he was surprised that he had not wondered before, and that knowledge had been so long denied.

He got up at last, and looked at his reflection in the mirror. He saw an oldening, flaccid face with live eyes, and a grey jowl that needed shaving; and he slapped that slack jowl and said:

'T'hell with it! I'll not shave this morning.' And he did not.

He gave himself the rudiments of a wash and a brush, donned an old tweed suit, and hesitated for minutes before going downstairs to a standard breakfast similar to forty thousand that had gone before: grape-fruit, kidney and bacon, morning rolls, and thin coffee. His wife was already at the table, her morning paper propped as usual on the coffee-pot. She was still a good-enough-looking woman going thin, and already, this early in the morning, she was coiffeured and powdered and lip-sticked to face another strenuous day similar to the forty thousand social days that had gone before. She spoke casually without lifting her eyes from the paper.

'You were late last night, my old truant—' She glanced at him, and stopped. Then she tapped the table schoolma'am fashion and her voice hardened, 'Drunk or sober, I will not have you in my breakfast-room like that. Go back and shave!'

'I just worked it out,' said Sean equably. 'Three years four days and forty minutes I have wasted in shaving.'

'A cold bath will sober you—'

'Sober as a judge, and looking at you soberly,' said Sean. 'Woman, you look like the wrath o' God under pink and white buckram. Pour me a cup of that thing you call coffee!'

'Do you hear me, Sean?' Her voice was dangerously mild.

'Not to heed you. Coffee, please!'

'I will not—certainly not till you shave.'

'Oh yes! you will,' said Sean and walked slowly round the table to her.

'Don't be a silly old fool at your time of life!' She tried to dominate him with her eye as was her habit, but, to her silly old fool, her eye was now only cold china-blue.

'Let's try it this way,' said Sean.

Very carefully but shrewdly he slapped her left cheek with his right palm, and restored the balance by slapping her right cheek with his left palm.

'Coffee, please!' said Sean.

And she was so astounded that, before she had time to flame, she poured coffee, filling cup and saucer, with some over for the table mat. And her flame, when it came, would not scorch a fly. She was on her feet and making for the door.

'You will hear from my solicitor,' she said. 'I am going to my daughter's.' That might be an adequate threat for suburbia, but not for Sean any more.

'Don't bother yourself!' said Sean, and gulped some lukewarm coffee.

Thereafter Sean went to town, and in more ways than one. He did not drive his big American car, but took an eightpenny bus amongst members of the lower middle class, who are only noted for their self-conscious inferiority.

His lady-secretary had his morning mail ready for him in his comfortable office, but he did not even glance at it or her. He sat down and wrote to himself, as Managing Director, a letter resigning his Chairmanship. It was a thoroughly abusive letter.

Then he made a holograph will, and left everything to some society that, for all the good it did, might be a society to provide blind kittens with dead mice.

And as a final gesture he went out to his select golf club, hauled his five-guinea golf bag to a secluded part of the course, and, with gusto, wrapped four woods and fourteen graded irons round the trunk of a handy ash sapling. He then set a lighted match to the empty bag, after pelting a dozen new balls at a scolding magpie. For a minute he was in two minds whether he should set another lighted match to the clubhouse, but decided against it on the ground that every member was entitled to his own hell.

That was the end of Sean in business and social circles. Never again was hair or hide of him seen where folk worship respectability. He disappeared into the unknown, and every effort to trace him failed. After seven years his death was legally assumed, and in the subsequent dispute over his holograph will the legal profession gorged itself like a vulture.

But Sean was far from dead. He had never been more alive in his life. Neither did he disappear. He merely changed his habitat. He went out into the width of the country, and lived close to the ground amongst men and women sib to him. He knew hunger and thirst and the satisfying thereof; he saw the sun rise and the sun set; he slept under the moon and the stars; he felt the rain and the wind and the sun; he lived.

Sometimes he walked alone; sometimes he marched with the tinker clan; sometimes he rode with the caravanners. And there was a tinker woman too, who robbed with him from door to door, county to county, sea to sea. Let a veil be drawn. . . .

At the age of ninety Sean had another change of mood. His Faith was restored to him. He married his fourth tinker woman, and died in the odour of sanctity within the year.

If this cautionary story has a maxim, it is that every man should have a Fairy-Godmother.

THOMASHEEN JAMES GOES TO THE DOGS

IT was one Isaac Watts that sang: 'For Satan finds for idle hands some mischief still to do.' I am setting out to prove that.

I was at a loose end that afternoon. My family was at the seaside in far-away Kerry; my man-of-no-work, Thomasheen James, *alias* Satan, might or might not be pottering in some sheltered recess of the garden; and I, in a deck-chair on the patch of lawn fronting the summer-house, was failing to put a useful sentence on a writing-pad. The soothing June sun would put me asleep in about two minutes. It did not.

Thomasheen James's peeled and freckled face lifted above a berry bush, and his high-pitched voice twisted an old saw to his own liking.

'Did you ever hear the old saying: when the cat's away to play the mouse goes the same way? You did not.'

'Never,' I said. 'Who is the cat?'

'Any female woman of the opposite sex, and I'll go no nearer than that.'

'And I'm the mouse?'

'What else—the same as any married man under the sun, moon, and stars. As you say yourself, there's only one man to carry freedom under his hat—and a dam' bad hat it is. But I'll not be boastin'.'

He rose to his feet, slipped between the berry bushes, and came out on my patch of lawn. His galluses looped to his knees, and his grey shirt-sleeves, stagged off at the elbows, showed his tanned and wiry forearms. He propped his pointed chin on the end of a garden rake, rubbed his sandy poll under a tweed hat that had once been mine, and contemplated me with a possessive eye. I was his meat and I knew it. For a dozen years he had used me for his own purposes and my occasional profit, and there was nothing I wanted to do about it. His voice was remote.

'Do you know what I'm thinkin'?'

'I will not,' I said firmly.

'You'll not what?'

'I'll not fall in with any of your suggestions.'

'I'm not suggestin' nothin',' he protested warmly. ''Tis how I had it in me mind that you and me, the both of us, might go to the dogs for the evenin'.'

'Are you proposing a pub-crawl?'

'Be the powers! That's an idea. I'm fam'lar with a crawl that will land us contagious to a taxi-stand, and I'll see you safe home in bed, your shoes off, and ne'er a collar-stud to strangle your windpipe. No! I promised the missus not to lead you into temptation and deliver you from all evil amen. The dogs I had in mind was the running dogs at Shelbourne Park.'

'And what do you use for money?'

'That's a leadin' question, sure enough. Owin' to penur'ous resources, me financial condition is no credit to the man concerned, and I'm naming no names. But if I had a single, solitary one-pound note for a sinewy war—.'

'Drunk, disorderly, and ten days hard—with the option of a thirty-shilling fine to be paid by me.'

'Drink never tangled my feet in the course o' business,' said Thomasheen James with dignity. 'First and foremost I'd peregrinate on me two feet down be the Quays and consultate me old butty, Davy Hand—.'

'Not with a pound of mine in your pants,' I said warmly.

Davy Hand is a little Dublin Jackeen, a breeder of fighting dogs and fancy canaries, and when he and Thomasheen James join forces it is time for honest citizens to take cover. Thomasheen James ignored my interruption.

'The world knows Davy Hand has no more brains in his head than a hen crossing the road in front of a truck, but he has resources of information where dogs is concerned.'

'Fighting dogs.'

'Ay, and running dogs as well! Look at here! Davy is brother-in-linked arms to one of them white-coated lads that do be parading the dogs on the track; and that's the buckeroo that has his finger on the right prime hound to come out of the ruck at the last bend at six to one, maybe more. Are you listenin'?'

'Not interestedly.'

He walked across the grass and back again on the balls of his feet, and made a sweeping gesture towards a horizon where fortune waited.

'Give me wan hour with Davy Hand, and the writing will be close to the wall.' He faced me squarely and shook a clenched paw. 'As sure as small potatoes and few in the drill, I'll be on the look-out for you at the car-park, and if I haven't two winners, I'll have four.' He thrust an itching persuasive palm at me. 'A pound note for a sinewy war, me gallant man?'

'You don't get it, my gallant man,' I said coldly. 'But you can develop your sinews staking peas.'

2

Need it be said, I went to the dog-races that evening. My wife had not taken her car to Kerry, and I used it. Thomasheen James had disappeared an hour previously so 'rencontre' his butty, Davy Hand, and, need it be taid, a pound note of mine reposed in his pants pocket as his sinews of war.

I looked for him in the car-park outside the race-track, but he was not there. I waited ten minutes, and then resignedly bought me a ticket to the main enclosure, for I now knew that my incubus was on a ploy of his own, and that I would not see him for four hours or four days, at the end of which time he would meticulously explain the loss of my pound or the winning and spending of ten.

I was not greatly interested in the races that evening. The barefaced, rough-shouldered cupidity of the dog-racing addicts repelled me, and I was missing Thomasheen James. He has no luck in picking winners, but he is good company, and his explanation of misfortune long before misfortune arrives always keeps me guessing, and guessing wrong.

It was some time before the fifth race that my interest came alive. I was moving slowly along the line of bookmakers on the rails watching their boards and trying to feel a hunch for some particular dog. A man was strolling casually ahead of me. He was a tall, slender man with a sleek, bare black head and wearing easy fitting but well-cut grey flannels—a man of some distinction in looks, but not conspicuous in any way.

He paused before a bookmaker, nodded familiarly, extended a flat wad of notes, and mentioned a dog's name. I did not catch that name. By the size and clean whiteness of the notes he tendered I knew them for a Bank of England issue. And it was there my interest came alive, for I remembered something about Bank of England notes, something that my friend, Detective-Inspector Joe O'Dowd, had told me in confidence some days before.

Before turning away, the tall man glanced in my direction. Perhaps he saw the interest in my eyes, for he hesitated and frowned before moving off. Having seen his face and eyes, I knew his race. He was a lean member of that race, his nose aquiline but not fleshy; it was the set and colour of his eyes, the strong teeth, the firm yet voluptuous mouth that told me of his breed. I moved after him.

Four places down he again bet a wad of Bank of England notes, and again he glanced at me. This time he did not frown, but I definitely did not like the half-hidden look in his eyes. In ordinary circumstances I would have left him then, but my interest in those white Bank of England notes drew me in his footsteps.

He made a third bet, and this time he faced round and took two paces towards me. He smiled, and his voice was low and well modulated.

'My good sir, if you are interested in that dog, its name is Benmee, and put your shirt on it.'

'No interest in it whatever,' I said.

He had smiled at me, but his eyes belied the smile. Catch that lizard-look in any man's eyes, get out from under, and call on your guardian angel.

With a lithe sinuousness he slipped away amongst the crowd, and I was left with a cold sensation running down my spine. What I should have done then was to phone Inspector Joe O'Dowd from the Secretary's office. I might have done so had not an eager voice spoken in my ear.

'Did you hear the buck? Benmee, and it five to one this bleedin' minute. And look at here! That's the very same identical dog that Davy Hand swore me to secrecy. I' been lookin' for you. Have we e'en a shirt atween us?' That was Thomasheen James.

'I wouldn't put a shilling on it,' I said, 'to save my immortal soul.' And I left him.

Benmee won that race by lengths, but the odds had come down to two to one against before the traps lifted. I had no more bets. In fact, I had had only two the whole evening, and came out a little on the right side.

3

Thomasheen James was waiting for me outside the gate of the park. He beckoned me out of the press, and was inclined to be petulant.

'She'll be back to you, won't she?' he said.

'Who?'

'The wife, and who else? Sure if your brain wasn't wanderin' in the wilds o' Kerry you'd have your last gallus button on Benmee.'

'You had?'

'Our noble pound went on its nose at fives. Look at that!'

He extracted from his hip-pocket a crumpled but clean white note. He smoothed it out and patted it affectionately, and I saw that it was a five-pound Bank of England note.

'That's the rale article,' he said. 'Good from here to Timbuctoo!'

'Probably not worth the paper it's engraved on,' I told him.

'Hoo-hoo-hoo!' he derided. 'The wan and only docyment in financial circles you could back your immortal soul on.'

'And lose it.'

A voice spoke behind my left shoulder.

'Say, my lad, I'll give you an Irish fiver for that Bank of England note.'

I did not turn round, but I knew that cultivated and well-modulated voice. I kept my eyes on Thomasheen James. His mouth was open in astonishment, but already in his china-blue eyes was the cunning that saw profit round the corner.

'A dirty Irish fiver!' he said, and folded his note once.

'I cross to London to-morrow,' explained that cool voice, 'and Irish notes are not popular over there.'

'Glad I'd be to faciliate a gentleman,' said Thomasheen James. 'But—'

'I get your point,' said the other, chuckling. 'Fair enough! A fiver and a single for that note?' I heard the rustle of paper behind me.

Thomasheen James's hand was on the reach when I acted. I do not think I willed that act. I just acted.

'I might need that fiver too,' I said, picked it out of Thomasheen James's finger, folded it again, and thrust it into a trouser pocket.

The man behind laughed lightly. 'You are welcome, my friend,' he said. He brushed by my shoulder, and I watched him move along the flank of the crowd in his graceful sinuous way.

Thomasheen James was speechless for an appreciable time, and was almost at the hand-wringing stage. And when his voice came it was thin and strangled with emotion.

'Luv! it must be luv! What else would madden a man to take a pound note out of me pocket?'

People were glancing at us, and I did not want a scene. I turned on my heel and said:

'Do you want a lift?'

'No!' he almost shouted, and steadied himself. 'I got commitments I can't fill no more.'

I left him then. I knew that his 'commitments' were to Davy Hand, and that he lacked a fiver to fulfil them. But he would have at least his original capital, and that would go some distance. I assumed that I would not see Thomasheen any more that night.

I drove leisurely into town, and had supper at the Dolphin Bar, for I was in no hurry home to my empty house. At that hour of the evening the immense horseshoe curve of marble counter was not half-filled, and most of the clients were dog-racing fans.

I was sampling a dry sherry before supper when

again I heard that cool cultivated voice behind me.
It had a curt note in it this time.

'You grub at the other end. I'll pay.'

And a rough but servile voice made answer.

'Whatever you say, Mr Segor.'

The footsteps moved away, and I turned my head
aside to look. Yes, that was my slender, sleek-haired
man in well-cut flannels, and apparently his name was
Segor. He took a stool six or eight places down, and
did not once glance in my direction.

His two myrmidons—they looked like that—went
along to the end of the bar. One was a heavily built,
smooth-faced, thick-jowled fellow, and he had thug
written all over him; the other, broken-nosed,
raddle-faced, looked depraved even beyond thugdom.
I looked at that seond man again, and I knew him.

I have, in another place, related the misadventure of
Thomasheen James and the Opprobious Name: how
one Barney Doony, ex-soldier, ex-showman, had been
the bane of his life for twenty years; how finally he had
committed mayhem on Doony in the town of Ard-na-
Righ; and how the subsequent court proceedings cost
me three pounds in fines.

That second man was Barney Doony of ill-fame.
He may have recognised me too, but he gave no
sign.

I had supper. For a time I considered ringing up
Inspector Joe O'Dowd, but what had I to show him:
a Bank of England five-pound note that might or
might not be genuine; and I could not say that our
Mr Segor had ever held that note. I decided to sleep
on it, and consult Joe O'Dowd in the morning. I paid

my bill and went out to my car. I left Segor and his men in the bar, but Segor, too, was paying his bill as I left.

It was eleven o'clock in the half-dark of a salubrious summer night when I got to my own gate. Driving up the short avenue between the clipped impressive hedges I saw that the front of the house was in darkness, as it should be, and that no light showed in Thomasheen James quarters back of the garage—I did not expect to see any. It was as I shut the garage door that sounds came that made me leap in my tracks and swear. Semi-musical but raucous voices came from the rear of the house, and I seemed to recognise the tune of *Hanagan's Ball*.

'In the town of A-thy one Jeremy Hanagan
Battered away till he hadn't a pound
His uncle he died, and made him a man again,
Left him three cows and an acre of ground.'

'Hell's bells!' I said. Thomasheen James and Davy Hand singing in what they call unity. They're in the kitchen and the house on fire.'

I bruised a shin on Thomasheen James's barrow at the gable-end, hopped forward on one leg, and flung the kitchen-door wide. The electric bulb under the ceiling lit a scene that was not yet fully bacchanalian. There were, indeed, a dozen or more beer bottles on the table, but not more than six empty ones on the floor. The party had not yet got into its stride. And before I could get into mine, Thomasheen James took the floor. He faced me, a half-empty beer bottle held like a torch, and his voice made proclamation.

'Me gallant friend, the drinks is on me; the produce

73

of me own bow and arrow, the juice of the barley grain extricated be the application of my acquaintance with runnin' dogs, be the agency of David Hand heretofore present. The resources of this noble house is still entire.'

Here Davy Hand shouldered him aside. Davy, that breeder of fancy canaries and fighting dogs, was a short tubby little wastrel, and conservative in attire. Winter and summer, indoors or outdoors, he wore a rusty-black overcoat tightly buttoned over a round paunch, and a black bowler hat resting securely on generous ears.

'Me dear sir,' he said, 'this baster' has no more manners than me foot in the house of a right friendly gentleman.' Here he struck his breast as in deep contrition. 'The heart is melted in me that you wasn't able to take advantage of the one and only sure thing I had for you to-day. But who am I to question your conclusion, for it could be that you had a sound reason of your own which the same I freely acknowledge—'

Thomasheen James, in turn, shouldered Davy aside and faced me, dignity in posture and voice.

'Me gallant sir, you discommoded me business relations with a certain gentleman unnamed, but I'll say nothing about that in me ginerous nature. But cast your memory back? In the afternoon of the present evening you loaned me a hesitating one-pound note—'

'Loaned?'

'The signifying word on a business occasion.' He moved a hand forward. 'You have the gem of all fivers in your pants pocket, and if you happen to have

74

four singular ones handy, after a riotious evenin', reach
'em to me and all obligations are cleared between us,
past, present, and to come in the future. Am I right?'

Any anger there was in me had evaporated. It
always did.

'It is after business hours,' I said, and took the Bank
of England note from my pocket. I unfolded it,
smoothed it out, examined it under the light, and
held it up against the light. It looked a perfectly
genuine note to me, and the metal filament seemed to
be in the right place. But I was not an expert.

'That's a five-pound note, if your education is
neglected,' said Thomasheen James.

'Who gave you this, Mr O'Doran?' I asked him.

'Who gave me this?' His voice thinned derisively.
'In words out of the ha'penny book I bet a pound note
value twenty shillings that a certain racing dog, be
name Benmee would win the fifth race at fives, the
venoo being Shelbourne Park in this city, and the
bookmaker Jock Morton, prince of the ring. As a
raysult the aforesaid Jock extended me that five-pound
note, and me own pound additional,' he gestured
towards the table, 'which I have expended for the
entertainment of man and beast in this house. Is that
clear?'

'Not very,' I said. Morton was the last bookmaker
with whom I had seen Segor lay a bet, but that proved
nothing. Thomasheen James had his hand thrust
forward.

'If you can't change that note to-night due to pro-
fligation, hand it over to me, and I'll do the needful
first thing in the morning.'

75

'N-o-o!' I said musingly. 'No, I don't think so.
I'll hold this to-night, and consult a higher authority
to-morrow.'

I was looking down at the note, and committing
the serial number to memory. I did not notice the
hush that came over Thomasheen James and Davy
Hand, and I had not heard any sound from behind.
And again that cool slow voice spoke.

'Not to-morrow, my friend.' The voice crisped.
'Put them up! Up with them all of you!'

Thomasheen James's and Davy's hands were already
in the air. I felt something touch the crawling muscles
in the small of my back, and my arms went up too, the
bank note in the fingers of my right hand.

A hand came over my shoulder and plucked the note
away. Then I was shoved forward, not forcefully,
between Thomasheen James and Davy, and the voice
said :

'Turn round now!'

I turned round. My man in flannels, Segor, folded
the banknote, put it in his wallet and restored the
wallet to an inner breast-pocket. He was not looking
at me, had no weapon in either hand, and I might have
leaped at him. I did not. At his left, and a little
behind, stood Barney Doony. He had no weapon
either, but the lewd grin on his broken mouth was
nearly as bad. I heard Thomasheen James growl in
his throat, and his head was thrust forward.

At Segor's right hand, and a little in front stood the
heavy jowled thug, and he was armed—and more than
ready. A flat automatic moved back and forth like
the head of a snake, and the glazed eyes of a killer

gave their own message. But, somehow, I was not really afraid, for chagrin at my own folly subdued all other feelings. Why, oh why, had I not phoned Joe O'Dowd?

The man lifted his eyes and smiled at me, quite a pleasant smile.

'Simple, wasn't it?' he said softly, and brushed one hand over the other in a cleansing motion.

I said nothing, but I was in complete agreement.

'You are not a policeman, I know,' he went on in that cool voice, and tapped over his breast-pocket. 'You were very interested in this note. What are you going to do about it now?'

'Nothing—yet,' I said then.

'Nothing—ever,' he corrected. 'To-night you will do nothing, and to-morrow is another day. What have you got to show?'

I had nothing to show, but before I could admit it, Thomasheen James threw his hat in the ring.

'Say, me dear misther man,' he said in his pleasantest voice, 'you'll not be forgetting that you owe me six Irish quid?'

His dear mister man laughed just as pleasantly.

'I offered you six pounds, my fool,' he said, 'and your friend or boss intervened. He owes you your six quid, and see that you get it.'

'Do you mane to say—?' Gun or no gun, Thomasheen began exploding.

'I have said it. Shut up!' And the new rasp in that voice effectively silenced Thomasheen James. Even at that rather tense juncture I told myself that I must practise that rasp for self-protection.

The man Segor took one step forward, and turned his attention to me; and again I saw that lizard-look in his eyes. He gestured towards the beer bottles on the table.

'I will not detain you from your hog-swilling,' he said smoothly. 'Just one small token to remind you to mind your own business.'

And before I could move my hands to guard he smashed his open hand along my jaw and cheek. I went sideways, but Davy Hand's arm and shoulder brought me upright again. And then Thomasheen James went berserk.

'Waugh!' Thomasheen James yelled his warcry, and leaped at Segor. That man stepped back nimbly, and I thought Thomasheen James a dead man as the thug's gun came forward. But no! As Thomasheen landed in front of Segor, the thug hit him with gun and fist above the ear and Thomasheen James went down at my feet.

He has a hard head, Thomasheen, and the blow was not heavy enough to be lethal. Already he was scrambling to his feet, and there I took a risk myself, for I would not have my poor fool manhandled any more. As he reached his feet I brought my hands down, grasped him round the shoulders, and held him firmly against me.

Segor's voice was as cold and clear as spring-water. 'Care to try anything, tubby?' That was to Davy Hand. 'No! Then the session is over. Attention please! If anyone goes outside this house for the next hour he will be responsible for his own death. that's all. Good-night, and drink your woes under!'

He turned carelessly on his heel and went out into the night. Barney Doony, leering, followed him. The thug went out backwards, his gun ready. He paused in the doorway, and his voice came in a husky inviting whisper.

'Don't mind the boss! Yer welcome to step out any time. I need the practice.'

The door banged. Davy Hand's arms were still in the air. Now they dropped helplessly to his side, and he heaved a long breath.

'I wonder am I dead or waking up to-morrow mornin'?' he wanted to know, and sank weak-kneed into a Windsor chair.

I pulled Thomasheen's head round. There was a trickle of blood by his ear, but the wound was only a scratch. I tried to lead him to the kitchen, but he resisted.

'I'm all right!' he said. 'The only thing the matter with me is everything.'

He caught my wrists fiercely and looked into my eyes. His own eyes were blazing yet anguished, and the tears were running down his cheeks.

'He hit you,' he whispered in torment. 'He hit you, he hit you. Wan friend of me heart, he hit you. Oh God! oh God! I'll live a thousand years, and rind him limb from limb.'

'Don't be a dam' fool,' I said huskily. 'Sit down there!' I thrust him into another chair, and he crouched forward, his head between his hands. My cheek was stinging, but I did not mind that. What I could barely stand was a feeling of complete abasement. But I had to stand that too, and do the only thing possible at this eleventh hour. I cleared my throat and spoke in a monotone to keep my voice steady.

'Lock the back door, Davy, and pull down that blind. I am going to do what I should have done four hours ago.'

I opened the door leading into the house, went up three steps, and along a dark passage to the front hall, where the telephone was. With the aid of a match cupped in my palm I dialled the number I wanted, got the double buzz, and waited in the darkness.

'Hullo! who is speaking?' That was Joe O'Dowd's wife.

'Hullo, Kitty! Is Joe back?'

'Is it yourself, sir? He has the usual small game in the backroom. Are you coming out?'

'Not to-night, Kit. I want to speak to Joe. Tell him it might be important.'

'At once, sir.'

And in ten seconds Joe's southern voice was in my ear.

'Important is it?'

'It might be. I've been a dam' fool, Joe.'

'That's not important. Evidence please.'

'Listen! You told me some time ago that your opposite number at New Scotland Yard passed word that an international gang might be unloading counterfeit Bank of England notes in Dublin?'

'Yes, I told you that. Go on!' There was a new note in his voice.

'I saw wads of Bank of England notes being unloaded on the bookmakers at Shelbourne Park this evening.'

'You didn't think of phoning me there and then?'

'That's where I was a dam' fool, Joe.'

'Easy, my son, easy!' he said softly. 'Many's the time I've been a dam' fool myself. Is that all?'

'I had one of the notes in my hands. It looked all right to me.'

'Of course! Only two small defects for the expert. Have you that note now?'

'It was taken away from me five minutes ago.'

'Where?' His voice grated.

'In this house.'

'A hold-up?' he whispered.

'By a very dangerous man, and a warning not to leave the house for an hour.'

'Now that is important. I'll be with you in fifteen minutes.'

'Be careful. The house is watched.'

'I don't think so, but I'll be careful. I'll come the back way across your paddock. When you hear me tap once and then twice on the kitchen door, put out the light before opening up. And look here! Stand yourself a good ball o' malt and get rid of that strain.'

I went into the dining-room, switched on the light, put a bottle of gold-label whiskey and four glasses on a tray, and went back to the kitchen.

'We need something stronger than cold beer,' I said.

'God share you the health!' said Davy Hand warmly.

Thomasheen James, head down, said nothing.

I poured three stiff whiskies and added a little water from the sink. Davy Hand sampled his drink daintily; I swallowed mine in two gulps; Thomasheen James tossed his straight down on the pit of his stomach, shivered through all his being, and looked up at me. His eyes were washed out now, and he shook a doleful head.

'Man, dear,' he said, 'me and you, the both of us, had some gallant adventurings in our time, but sure every man has to meet his Waterloo.'

'This fight is not over yet,' I said. 'Joe O'Dowd is on the way.'

'That's the fellow'll lock the stable door nice an' handy,' said Thomasheen James bitterly, and again sank into depressed musings.

We waited, mostly in silence. Though I was listening intently for Joe's double tap, when it came I jumped a foot. He crawled in on his hands and knees. I locked the door behind him, and again switched on the light. On his feet he looked with some surprise at Thomasheen and Davy, and pointed a thumb from one to the other.

'Keep your voices down. Which do I pull in? Both?'

For once Thomasheen James had no come back. Detective-Inspector Joe O'Dowd was a big-shouldered, flat-stomached, smooth-faced man in loose tweeds, and with a disreputable Irish hat half-hooding his live eyes. He shoved beer bottles aside, sat on the edge of the table, and nodded at me pleasantly. I think he saw the trouble in my eyes.

'Take it easy, my son!' he said. 'We have not much time to waste as I see it. Tell me everything you have as concisely as possible, but miss nothing out. Carry on!'

And as is my habit I walked back and forth from wall

to wall as I talked. And I missed nothing out. He did not interrupt me once, but occasionally he nodded, and occasionally under the leaf of his hat I saw his eyes light up.

'That is all,' I said at the end, and leant against the corner of the white electric cooker.

Joe O'Dowd rasped his firm chin and shoved his hat back on his head. After a while he spoke consideringly.

'Yes, that is important, and it takes us so far. Your Mr Segor—that is not his name of course—beyond a doubt he was unloading snide notes, and made his killing this evening; and he is getting out pronto, for to-morrow is another day, as he said. Bank of England notes have been suspect for some time, but that lad would have his own technique for winning confidence, and I can assume it for you. For a month or longer he would be going to every race-course and dog-track in the vicinity of Dublin, laying bets with selected bookmakers. All genuine bets and genuine notes. A pony on here, a pony on there, winning a little losing a little, but all the time winning confidence. And when the time was ripe and a certain dog ready, he made his killing. That was this evening.'

Joe moved a hand towards me. 'You saw him lay a good wad of notes three times, but he probably laid more that you did not see. He would pull down anything from five to ten thousand pounds, and he is making his getaway. Be sure that he has his line of retreat open : a private plane, a motor cruiser anchored off-shore, a fast car by an unauthorised road over the Border—how do I know? All I do know is that if I

do not get him within an hour or two I do not get him
at all.'

'How do you get him?'

'Through the one mistake he made. Even the
cleverest crook makes his one mistake, otherwise where
would we come in? You see, he was perturbed by
your interest in his bets, and by the way you picked
Thomasheen James's fiver from under his nose. After
that he watched you like a hawk, and trailed you everywhere you went, making sure you contacted no one.
And then he made his mistake. He was so sure of his
getaway that he thought he would relieve you of that
fiver, and at the same time teach you a lesson. That
was his mistake, for it tied a string to him.'

'What string?'

'Barney Doony,' said Joe O'Dowd.

'Waugh!' That was Thomasheen James coming
alive.

'I don't see it,' I said.

'I don't see it very clearly myself,' admitted Joe,
'but it is there. You see, we know nothing about
Segor or where he hangs out. We know nothing about
his gunman either. But we do know about Barney
Doony. I have a file that thick on him. Ex-soldier,
ex-pug, ex-showman, racing tout, tick-tack man,
bookie's runner, petty criminal, I can pull him in any
time to-morrow, but it will be too late then, and he'll
have dam' little to tell.'

The policeman got to his feet and faced Thomasheen
James and Davy Hand. He thrust an urgent hand at
them.

'Come on boys! Snap out of it. We are this far, and

we are bound to go farther. Give me a lead on Barney
Doony. There must be something, any little thing at
all.'

Thomasheen James rose out of his chair. On the
balls of his feet he went acrouch across the room and
back again, one arm a-swing and the other cocked for
an uppercut.

'Barney Doony! the rap that put an opprobious
name on me! Barney Doony that I absquatulated in
Patsy Kelleher's bar, livers and lights on the floor and
a dint in his poll you could whip a salad in—'

Suddenly he pulled himself upright, and spread his
arms wide. 'Wo, mare, wo there!' Slowly and on
tiptoe he approached Davy Hand, who was staring at
him open-mouthed. He closed Davy's mouth with a
smart tap under the chin, shoved his bowler hat back,
and put a tightly clenched fist under the little man's
nose.

'You runt of a remnit of a dishonest dog-stealer!
Have you lost every scrap of memory the divil leant
you behind a back door. What do you raycall about
Barney Doony?'

Davy moved Thomasheen James's hand aside.
'Didn't I try to pi'son him wan time with a quart of
stale porter and ten drops o' croton oil in it? You might
as well try to excavate a truck.'

'Holy Moses! The fright has addled his brains.'
Thomasheen James's voice coaxed him. 'Listen, me
little boy! would you capitulate your last dishonest
transaction with him?'

'Begod!' said Davy Hand sitting up.

Joe O'Dowd's urgent hand warned me to be still.

This was Thomasheen James's innings, and Thomasheen James went on making runs.

'And tell me now and tell me no lie, was it a month or six weeks ago you sold Barney a watchdog—that Kerry Blue bitch, ten year old, wouldn't bite a dint in a pat of butter?'

'She was a good bitch wan time.'

'Wan time is right. And to proceed, what did Barney want the bitch for? Take your time now!'

Davy's mouth opened and shut. He rose suddenly to his feet, pushed Thomasheen James aside, and advanced a couple of paces.

'The cute divil has something there, Inspector Joe. I sold Barney the bitch—Juno be name—but he was only acting for a gintleman rentin' a remote house in a lonely part of the county.'

'You know this remote house, Davy?' asked Joe O'Dowd quietly.

'Why not I? I delivered the bitch. I had to. She wouldn't be led or drove by Barney, and took a lump out of his collop to show her intintions—and that was no pat of butter whatever.'

'Where is this house, Davy?'

'Foxrock,' said Davy.

Foxrock is only eight miles out of Dublin, and one of its most select suburbs; but to Davy Hand, living in a rabbit-warren tenement, it would be a wilderness of loneliness.

'You would know the house again, Davy?' queried Joe softly.

'Day or dark. Three houses th'other side of the railway station, maybe four; a granite-built house with a red roof an' a white gate, and a big monkey-puzzler growin' on the front lawn.'

'Did you see anyone about?'

'Nary a wan. Barney thrun me out prompt after tyin' up the bitch.'

Joe O'Dowd turned to me grimly.

'There's our string. Care to see what's at the other end?'

'If I may,' I said mildly.

Thomasheen James hopped on the floor.

'The man that tries to stop me,' he challenged, 'I'll take a fall out of him if he was as big as a bullock of Bashin'.'

Davy Hand settled his hat firmly on his head.

''Tis about time for me to go home,' he said cheerfully.

'Not be two jugfuls,' Thomasheen James told him. 'You'll come along and ameliate that bitch dog, you varmint.'

'God ha' mercy on me,' prayed Davy fervently.

'I'll use your phone for two minutes,' said Joe O'Dowd.

4

We drove out to Foxrock in Joe O'Dowd's police car; and we went fast. Thomasheen sat behind, one hand holding on to Davy Hand. Once he touched his other hand on my shoulder, and I felt its tremor.

'You're not frightened, are you?' I said.

'That's me storin' energy for a pleasant event,' he whispered in my ear. 'I'm like a ravelin' lion this blasted minit.'

At that hour we had the southern highway mostly to

ourselves once we got outside the city. The summer night was its usual toneless half-light, and, besides, a moon in its second quarter was sailing in a serene sky along the sweeping curve of the Dublin hills.

And, then, I noticed ahead of us the tail light of a car that was going at our own pace, and, looking through the back window, I saw the dimmed lights of a car that kept its distance.

Six miles out we turned right on a narrower road. The car in front had taken the same turn, and the car behind followed round on our tail. Approaching the railway at Foxrock we slowed down to a mere purr, and Davy pulled down the side window.

'There's the station now,' he whispered throatily. 'The house is on the wan side. Go on—on—a bit more —a bit more—a bit yet—wo! There's your white gate—and it open, and you can see the monkey-puzzler toppin' the roof. God be good to us! and isn't bed a grand place to be in this minit.'

The car stopped right in front of the open gate, and close in.

Joe whispered, 'They'll make no rush getaway—if they are not gone already.'

We got out as noiselessly as we could, and gathered round the policeman by the side of a concrete pier. The car ahead had stopped within forty yards, and several figures got out and moved into the hedge. the car behind had disappeared into the station yard. Joe already had a powerful hand inside Davy's elbow.

'The house will be surrounded when I give the signal,' Joe whispered, 'but first Davy and I will "ameliate" that dog. Follow me and I'll post you safely until I want you. No danger at all.' I did not believe him.

'God be here! Hold on a minute!' pleaded Davy.

But Joe drew him forward inexorably, slipped by the gate pier, and went close into some shrubbery that I think was grisolina. Thomasheen James and I followed closely in that order. I have known Thomasheen to display cowardice, but not that night. Thus we went on by a grass or clay margin, and round the back of a big araucaria pine, what Davy had called a money-puzzler. There we stopped, and it was surprise as much as anything else that stopped us.

We could now see the front of the house at a rather acute angle. The front door was wide open, and a cone of light splayed out across the gravel. That cone of light showed the long wide nose of a powerful American car facing in our direction and by its side, on the gravel, lay a big yellow-leather bag. A bow window the other side of the door was lighted up.

I heard Joe O'Dowd draw in a very deep breath. He held it for a moment and then exhaled it in a sharp double whistle. He was a prompt man.

'A short cut, and I take it. You stay put!' he said over his shoulder, and ran slantwise for the door.

I probably would have obeyed orders and stayed put. Thomasheen James did not. He was right on Joe's heels and, after one moment of hesitation, I followed him. I am not brave at all, but in a pinch Thomasheen James and I have a foolish habit of sticking together. I forgot all about Davy Hand, and I did not see him again until all was over. Somewhere at the back of the house a dog barked, and was silent.

Joe took three stone steps in his stride, and another long stride into the hall. Thomasheen James was not far behind, and I paused in the open doorway. Joe paused too for a quick glance round. The hall was short and scantily furnished in a mere utilitarian way; a linoed stairs went up ten steps and turned on itself; there was a closed door at the back, a closed one on the left, and a closed one on the right; behind that one on the right was a lighted room.

A sound behind made me turn a startled head. Two men looked up at me, and one lifted a finger. I at once recognised two of Joe's squad and felt happier.

After that waiting pause things happened with astonishing speed. The door on the right opened and a man came out lugging two heavy leather bags. He was the gunman thug. He did not swear or speak at all, but his face stiffened into the killer's mask. He dropped the bags, and his right hand flashed towards the open lapel of his coat. It did not get there. Joe leaped and struck. He may have used a cosh, but I do not think so. Even with a bare fist that swinging downwards blow would hold a gorilla. The man went down with a head-bumping crash in front of the doorway, and Joe promptly stepped over him and into the room. All that did not take five seconds. I heard Joe's fighting voice quoting Specimen Jones.

'Don't let anybody hurt nobody!'

Thomasheen James hopped over the fallen man, flicked back at him contemptuously with a hard heel, and dodged to the left inside the door. I stepped over carefully and with more dignity, and was wondering how many of a gang Joe was holding up. There was only the smooth flannel-clad crook, Segor.

I moved to Joe's right side. He held a gun in a swinging right hand, not an automatic but a long barrelled service revolver. This was evidently a sitting room, and it was barely furnished after the manner of houses that are rented by the month. Segor faced us from the empty fireplace in the left wall, his hands stiffly at his side and his face cool and still. Barney Doony was not in the house at all that night. In fact, he never did sleep in the house, but, of course, he was picked up without difficulty next day.

There was a certain invitation in Joe's voice.

'Keep your hands where they are Mr Segor, but please yourself.'

Segor's face never changed from its austere rigidity, but he looked at me, and the reptile was unashamed in his eyes. He must have known then that his position was hopeless, but he would not yield an inch. There was a calculated note of indignation in his voice.

'Damn you! who are you to intrude?'

'Detective-Inspector Joseph O'Dowd—at the end of the game,' Joe said pleasantly.

'Your identity card?'

'Don't mind it for a moment,' Joe said.

'You have a search warrant?'

'Why? I'm pulling you in for petty larceny and assault. That will hold you, and I can search you and this house for the stolen note—I know its number. Anything else?'

There was nothing else. One of Joe's boys slipped by

my shoulder and circled out into the room to get behind Segor.

'Run a hand over him, Mike,' Joe ordered, 'but I don't think he's heeled. Snaffle him when you're ready.'

It was at this juncture that Thomasheen James cleared for action. He went forward in a crouch to face Segor, one tightly clenched fist swinging below his knee.

'Blast you, O'Doran!' Joe barked at him. ' Don't cover my line. Get back!'

Thomasheen took no heed.

'There's a small bit of a debt ownin' be a fri'nd, you yalla hound,' he said softly to Segor. 'We always pay our debts, and this is the first installation.'

His fist came up in a looping drive, and I heard the ugly squash of bone on flesh. Segor's head went back, his knees buckled, and Thomasheen leaped on him; they went down under the detective's feet.

It took us all of a minute to prise Thomasheen James from his vengeance, and in that brief time he had done his mightiest. Segor, pulled to his feet, showed a face that surprised me. The mask was gone and his face was abased, and it was debased. It was as debased as Barney Doran's. And I felt distressed and abased too.

That is enough of that. For my part the adventure was over, and I can be brief now. Joe O'Dowd, in the house and baggage that night and next day, found all the evidence he required. It included an abandoned cache of counterfeit notes under the floorboards in an attic.

We finished the night in my kitchen—Joe, Thomasheen, Davy, and myself—and we had a much-needed drink. We talked too much, and were inclined to boast some, but we avoided any reference to pusillanimity on Davy's part. At our second and final drink I began to extol on the laws of chance.

'It took three things to complete the case,' I said, 'and they had to dovetail perfectly. A crook had to be overconfident in securing a mere five-pound note; Davy Hand had to sell a dog some weeks ago to an incompetent thug; and Thomasheen James had to remember it at the vital time. All chance.'

Joe O'Dowd hooded an eye at me over Thomasheen James's head.

'That five-pound note is missing,' he said, 'and we need it to compare serial numbers. Segor hadn't his wallet on him, and we haven't found it—yet.'

Thomasheen James slapped his breast-pocket contritely.

'I do be notin' a loss o' memory sometimes, and it'll cost me money wan o' these days,' he deplored. 'Didn't I know the wallet was prime evidence, an' I secreted it off the skunk when I climbed him.'

'I saw you,' said Joe. 'Hand it over, and the case is closed. Thank you, Mr O'Doran!'

Joe found the missing note in the wallet, and other evidence besides. Thomasheen turned his back on him, looked at me, and looked down at his hands. I looked there too. In one hand he held out a brown Irish fiver, in the other a green single.

'The choosin' is with you, gallant friend,' he said

in a low voice, 'an' haven't I the ginerous nature?'
He moved the single note forward.

I shook my head. 'I wouldn't touch one of them
with a forty-foot pole.'

'I thought you wouldn't,' said Thomasheen James.
'I have no such scrupilosity meself, and, sure, isn't the
labourer worth his dishonest wages?'

THOMASHEEN JAMES AND THE
DICTATION MACHINE

I WAS sitting inside the open door of the summer-house out of the sun, using two forefingers and a thumb on a typewriter that should be in a museum—and, probably, had been. My garden called to me, but I had an article to finish, and persevered in an uncongenial task.

I knew, with small satisfaction, that Thomasheen James, my man-of-no-work, was somewhere in the vegetable patch indiscriminatingly decapitating weeds and young carrots with a Dutch hoe; and I also knew that he would not stay long with that job in the heat of the day.

Thomasheen James keeps the wheel of his precious barrow well greased, and I did not hear him arrive on the square of grass fronting the summer-house. It was his remote contemplative voice that waked me up.

'Good luck to the man, and he able to choose a job won't drown'd him in his own sweat! And another poor gom tilin' and moilin', and drenched from toe to heel!'

I leant back in my wicker-chair and considered my henchman, retainer, parasite, incubus—whatever one cares to call him. He was sitting on the tail of his empty barrow, his long chin propped on the handle of a Dutch hoe; an ancient tweed hat of mine was perched precariously far back on his sandy poll; a grey shirt was stagged off at the elbows to show his tanned and wiry forearms; and neither forearms nor lean freckled face showed any signs of toiling and moiling under the sun.

Thomasheen James is not and never was in my employ. A man of his wandering blood is not employable, and if, at certain periods, he forsakes the wanderer's road and attaches himself to me, there is nothing I want to do about it. Our relations are strictly informal and, indeed, casual, yet there is a tie between us that time or tide, stress or storm, misadventure or misunderstanding cannot break. We make a team.

I felt for my tobacco-pouch, and leisurely filled a pipe. Thomasheen James extracted a corncob from a vest pocket, and moved one finger. After the necessary hesitation I threw the pouch at him, and he caught it neatly.

'Little enough a fill of grass-cut tobaccy on a mortial hot day,' he said. 'Couldn't I be knockin' the cap off a bottle o' beer for you? I counted six in the cupboard at your arm's length.'

'Fine!' I agreed. 'Pour me a bottle—just one.'

'That's all I meant, dammit!' said Thomasheen James.

He is an artist to pour beer, watching the mounting head carefully, and letting no sediment trickle over. He took two minutes to it, and, with a courtly gesture, handed me the misted glass.

I sampled the nutty flavour, and Thomasheen James took one hesitant step towards his wheelbarrow. 'I would ask you to try one,' I said with regret, 'but you would sweat all the more digging that pea trench.'

'I'll chance the perspiration, and let the trench look after itself,' he said, and reached for his bottle.

The pouring ritual repeated, he again sat on the tail of his barrow, looked through the amber liquor, and sampled it daintily.

'God spare us the health,' he said, put the glass carefully between his knees, and lit his corncob.

Through the smoke I saw one china-blue eye fixed on me speculatively, and I knew, of old time, that he had some outrageous proposal to spring unawares. I smoked and sipped and waited.

He took four quick puffs, and pointed the bitten stem of the corncob at my typewriter.

'I noticed it before, all your fingers is thumbs,' he began.

'They serve.'

'But you have a tongue in your head, haven't you? —and don't I know it—a tongue to scorch the hide off a man, or tickle a woman's ribs. If, be any manner o' means, you could use your tongue instead of your thumbs—'

'Not on a typewriter.'

'Exactly, me good sir! Eggs-ackly! Though, as myself knows, some of your langwidge is hard enough to punch keys. But tell me this, did you never hear of a gadget called a dictation machine?'

'A dictation machine?'

'The very thing! You know, one of them cabinet affairs, about so high and that wide, with a snake of a twisted-wire tube ejecting out of the top, and a mouthpiece to it like a penny trumpet.' He jerked his thumb. 'You switch a lever affair that way, and talk any dam' nonsense you like into the mouthpiece, switch again and clap the trumpet to your ear, and begod sir! the box talks back at you word for word—a blasted bloomin' miracle.'

'Oh! you mean a dictating machine?'

'Isn't that what I said, a dictation machine?'

'What the devil do you know about a dictating machine?' I asked in some surprise. 'Wait! Who has been priming you?'

He ignored that leading question.

'Ho-ho-ho! What do I know about dictation machines? says you. What don't I know about dictation machines? says I. Didn't I never tell you?'

'You did not. When did you make this up?'

''Tis me past life stirring in me insides, an' maybe you wouldn't want to hear about it.' He dismissed the matter with a gesture.

'Very well!' I agreed. 'What about that pea trench?'

'Sure the day is young. In the cool of the evenin' me and you'll make the clods fly.'

'I thought I knew of all your misadventures,' I said resignedly. 'Very well! What about this dictating machine—and what is it leading up to?'

'Devil the thing!' avowed Thomasheen James heartily. He sat back comfortably into his barrow, drank some beer, and got his pipe going again. This is the story he told me, and there may be some truth in it.

. . . . .

I'm going back in the years (said Thomasheen James) an' stoppin' short a long way from here. London it was, that consarned city of bricks that takes a hould of you like a shemale spider.

The war was over, and there was me discarded from the Rile Navy with a third-class certificate that said ne'er a word of all I had done on the British Empire. I had a notion at the back of me mind that London might be due for a bit speculation in a business capacity, so I was stayin' temperary in the Union Jack Club for soldiers and sailors in Waterloo Road, with a few spondulicks in me pants to pay my way if I had to—an' I sometimes had.

Them days I was of an inquirin' disposition in the supayrior walks o' life—not knowin' at the time that there ain't any—and I had a habit of taking a saunter through the West End and beyant to cogitate how the top half o' the world lived in tile hats and biled shirts and hides bare-naked to the third knot in a woman's backbone countin' upwards. An' I come to the conclusion—very well, very well! I'm not guilty of no bad langwidge.

Well, sir! One evenin'—a fine sunny evenin', I mind it well—it was Holy Thursday before Easter, what the English call Maundy Thursday, them not bein' customated to Christian festival occasions. I had pinitrated out as far as Chiswick be the Thames, a genteel locality abandoned to the boorjoo, with tall red-brick houses, an' tall windows curtained agin the inquisition of over-friendly neighbours.

In all that gentility there was only one pub that I came across, a retirin' affair with the front door discreetly round the corner in a laneway. And I turned that corner, natural as drawin' breath, me intintion bein' to sample a half-pint of mild-and-bitter. But it wasn't no beer I sampled that evenin'.

For at that eyedintical period o' time, the swing doors bust wide open, and a projectile came ejecting through in the shape of a gourilla. It looked like a gourilla anyway, or a ourangootang—one of thim apes without no tail. There was six foot of him an' a foot to spare, an' humped shoulders like a barn door, an' arms hangin' down over his knee-caps. An' before I could move hand or foot the same two arms was wrapped round me three or maybe four times, and a bull's bellow bust the drum of me ear.

'Well caught an' held—an' a head o' steam in the biler!' That's what he bawled, for it was human after all.

I thought me last hour had come unbeknownst, and I nearly went flat on the pavement under the ton weight of him. But I was a hardy young fellow in the days o' me youth, and after two staggers and a coupla gerations I propped him up unsecure, and got me windpipe untangled.

'You are an inconveniance, me good sir,' says I, humourin' him, for I was in dread o' my life. 'But, all the same, what in hell do you think you're doing, you big baboon?'

By this time, judging by the alcoholaceous gravity of his breath, I recognised that the big fellow was soaked to the ears, and had no manslaughter in his mind—yet. 'The prop of a rock in a dirty land,' says he. 'I'll have the loan of your shoulder up this street and round the corner—or do you die now?'

'Up the street and round the corner it is,' says I

with placation, being of a ginerous nature, as well
you know, when the sheets is in the wind. 'But if you
don't behave yourself.' says I, 'I'll have to kick your
teeth in.'

'Do,' says he. 'I never liked the dam' things.'

So I untangled myself gradual, propped him under
the oxter, and away we went wide and aisy from
pavement to street and back again, and anyone that
saw us coming had a sudden busine's in another
direction. And it was then I noticed that me ould
chimp was lame of one leg, and not so dam' sound on
the other.

We took two round circles to circumvint the corner.
And there we were in a quiet side avenue, with small
houses on both hands standing on their own patch o'
ground. It was as quiet as an evenin' after rain, and no
place at all for a cannybal chief.

'Look out for the Gila Monster!' mumbled me
prime ape. 'That's me, and the name of my house
forbye.'

We were at it already, and, as sure as I'm tellin' you,
the name was on the fanlight over the hall door. An
ugly bit of a house, a hop-and-a-jump off the street,
across a scrap o' lawn desecrated be a castor-oil plant,
an' the grass not cut in a donkey's years.

At the gate I made a move to get out from under me
awk'ard situation, but he had a tentacle on me. 'Not
on your life!' says he. 'Come on in, I got a ten-bob
note somewhere.'

That ten-bob note was comin' to me, so I went
along, and propped him up two steps to the front door.

'Your latchkey, Mr Man?' says I then.

'Don't use one, blast yer eyes!' says he. 'I amuse meself layin' gins for bu'glars, and have four o' them buried in the backyard.'

And sure enough, a twist of the door-knob half tumbled us into a square of hall without any furniture in it and inches deep in a month's sweepin's. And from there we bumped our per'lous way round the back of a stairs to a green door that he kicked open with his middlin' sound foot. And there we were in a great big barn of a study jutting out into the back garden.

And begod sir! regard to that same garden, as I saw later on with me own two eyes, there was four mounds, six be two, that looked dam' quare to me doubtful nature.

It was a powerful big room, as I said, and good enough lighted by three windows that needed washing since Adam was a boy. There was lashin's of furniture, and an electric fire was goin' full blast in the middle of the room. And instead of a carpet there was any god's number of skin rugs, with heads and paws large as life, and eyes glarin' yalla blazes: bears and lineses, and tigers, and cheetez and zebras, and I don't know how many more; and every foot of the wall was hid below antlers and tusks and twisty horns skull attached; and between them trofees—as he called them— was slung every savage murdherin' weapon from tropical lands—every bloomin', bloody impliment to fit the killin' hand of man the desthroyer everlastin'. The shivers was running up and down me back a'ready.

And look you! in all that half acre of room there

was only two places where a man could sit down in comfort: one was a well-used divan couch in a corner, and the other a solid tub-chair at a flat desk under a window. Every place else, desk and chairs and sideboard and why-nots and what-nots, was scattered and cluttered and heaped and piled with books and papers and docyments world without end amen. And a nice layer of dust for antiquy effect.

Well, sir! the big fella thumped himself down on the divan, and I had a good look at him for the first time.

Gor! he was big, an' the suit o' pla'd Harris tweed on him would make a waistcoat for an elephant. An' he was old too. The face of him was like a sheepskin tanned be wind and weather, and it had as many knobs and hollows as the Connamara mountains. A black patch covered one eye, but the other green eye was as lively as a trout, with a twitch to it sometimes, and sometimes a quare twinkle to make fun of anything livin' or dead. The roof of his skull was as naked as a goose-egg, and it was circulated be a bushy fuzz of red and grey tangle. Do you see him sittin' there foreninst me like the King of the cannybal islands on his divan throne, and myself wonderin' if he mightn't be needin' a snack supper with yours truly the main dish.

He threw a half hundredweight o' fist in my general direction, and I jumped a foot. He bawled as if I was a mile away. 'Try the middle drawer o' that desk, you sandy son of a gun! There's a half-note in it somewhere.'

'Never mind, sir!' says I. 'Sure an Irishman is always willin' to help a richinorous over a stile.'

'Orders, blast you!' he roared. 'I have yit to kill my first Irishman.'

So I tacked this way and that way atween the skins, and pulled open the middle drawer, and I didn't expect to see no ten-bob note eyther. Listen to me now! an' be as dumbfounded as meself. A ten-shillin' note? A fistful of them, an' pound notes, an' fivers, an' tenners—the bottom of the drawer was paved with them. There was five hundred pounds in that drawer if there was a penny.

Well, sir! I inserted me two fingers that way to extricate a solitary ten-bob note, when he let another bellow out of him. 'I'll try you out first, you varmint. Shut that drawer!' And I shut it. Mind you, it was aisy enough for me to palm a note then and there, but you know me. I have me failin's, as you point out frequent, but you or no man can call me petty larceenious. I shut that drawer on an empty palm.

He was cogitatin' me curious out of a half-shut eye, and says I circumspect: 'To hell with your ten bob! Is there a girl in the house to make a mug o' coffee for a drunk an' incapable?'

'You're drunk all right,' says he. 'What girl?'

'The slavey,' says I, 'or is she the cook?'

He half rose on his props, and sat down again. He yowled.

'Mention a woman's name in this house—mention it again—again once more and you're fired.'

'Fired?' says I.

'You're hired be capture,' says he. 'The only way! A month is the limit, an' I always pay the funeral expenses.'

An' I couldn't tell whether his wan eyes was twinklin' with devilment or anticipation.

'Coffee let it be,' says he then, and threw a hand towards the door. 'Find a kitchen somewhere and make it!'

I did. You'd expect to find the kitchen like a pig's mess. It wasn't, for he was a cute old dodger, and used only a cup and a saucer, a plate, knife and fork and spoon, and left 'em under water in the sink: There was coffee and tea and sugar galore in this press and that press, and butter as well, and tins o' this an' that, but divil a scrap o' bread could I find anywhere.

To make a long story short I concocted a jug o' black coffee strong enough to lift the roof off his skull, and I took it in on a tray with the cup and saucer and a bowl o' sugar.

He was lyin' on his back when I came in, but he heaved himself up like a Clydesdale horse, forelegs first and a wrench behind.

'Sugar?' says I, polite.

'Never!' says he, and poured half the bowl into the jug. Then he stirred it with the end of a fountain pen he got out of his vest, and tipped the whole mug straight down his gullet. It was hot enough to scorch him to the nabel, but all he said was, 'Cold as a stone, you bloody Irisher! I'll try another.'

An' that, me dear sir, was my first introduction to A. H. Giles—A. H. Giles, and litherary circles.

Yes, sir! The great A. H. Giles himself. You've read his novels o' fiction—I seen you myself. So have I—forty of 'em. The grandest writer on top o' the world for grown men an' growin' boys. Contimplate his universal hero MacClinkey, the Glasgow-Irishman. There's a brick for you, and I ha' followed him from China to Peru, from the South Seas to the Pacific Ocean, from the heart of Africay to the tempests of a serayglio. Everywhere! If me and you could write like that—all right, all right! He's dead these years, and we're alive. Ay, dead! And so is his great rival Egber Walters, the wan man he cursed night an' day because he turned out a book in a fortnight.

And there was me hired compulsory, but willin', by A. H. Giles himself; an' we can now proceed by leaps and starts. Me curious nature made me hang on to see if he was man or baiste, and an occasional ten bob was an advance on me funeral expenses. And in the course o' time I enjoyed myself in a jepardious way, for there was no bite behind his bark so long as I could keep black coffee on the brew to drownd his howlin'.

He lived and worked and slept in that big barb'rous room, and I had the rest of the house to myself—a sittin'-room in front, and me choice of three furnished bedrooms upstairs. As an old batman I tidied things to my satisfaction with a deck-brush, an' worked out a system notable be the absence of my presence except on demand.

At ten in the morning I took his breakfast to him: a quart o' coffee and marmalade. No! there was no toast. He downed the coffee slap-bang, and spooned a two pound pot o' marmalade, and that was his breakfast. And then at eleven prompt he locked his door, and I was left to me own devoirs. I used hear him in there yowlin' curses at MacClinkey, an' Mac cursin' him back, an' sometimes his voice would go up high and sugary, an' that would be a hello-huloo girl from the Poloponesean Islands. For, you see, he had a habit of playactin' his choice characters in the story on hand.

At five o'clock in the afternoon he called it a day, some more coffee, gave himself a brush and a shake, and slung his hook, dot-and-carry-one, into the West End. So did I on another task, but let that be.

Sometimes he came home middlin' airly, an' sometimes late as bedam'd, and often enough he came home the day after to-morrow, but late or airly he always came home biled, and late or airly there was always a pot o' coffee simmering on the gas-ring for him.

I suppose I should have had the time of me life them days. But I dunoo! Nothin' to do, an' time to do it, London under me foot, an' a frequent half-note in me pants! But lookin' back on it now I reco'nise it was a wearin' job, body and sowl, with the tinterhooks of anticipation stuck in my gizzard all the time.

And now my story is comin' close to the wall. It began on Holy Thursday in April, and the beginnin' o' the end came on the Thursday before the August Bank Holiday. Yes, sir! I held that job down for three solid months.

I was rayposin' in the front room, where there was a elegant chair to fit me shoulder blades. The time was getting on for five, and the MacClinkey brawl was about over for the day. Coffee time was again approachin'. I roused meself by degrees, and it was then I heard a car stop at the gate.

I had wan pane of glass I could reconnoitre through, and I observed a long-legged lad protruding himself backways out of a baby car, and haulin' a big cardboard case strapped in two places after him. He came up the path whistlin', an' wan shoulder draggin' to the weight o' the case.

'You'll whistle th'other side of your mouth in about two minutes, me Saxon friend,' says I to meself.

Canvassing gents and salesmen was a reg'lar pastime with ould A. H., and, often enough, I laughed me fill at wan o' them buck-jumpin' for the street minus collar and tie.

I met this tall young fella at the front door, an' hesitated before leadin' him to the line's den. Somehow I liked the gallant looks of him, and thought I might try and save the nice pin-stripe suit he was wearin'. He grinned at me in a friendly way, and says he, sure of himself.

'Is the great A. H. on the premises, young-fella-me-lad?'

'He is, and again he is not,' I tells him. 'If you haven't no appointment your goose is cooked, and if you have your name is mud. Sling your hook while the goin' is good, young fella yourself!'

'Holy Jerusalem!' says he. 'Save us from Dublin' town in the region of Inchicore—and his adenoidals should ha' been excavated when he was a baby.'

'Be the powders o' war!' I comes back. 'If you wasn't run out o' Wicklow you spent six months in jail with an Arklow man.'

'I was and I did,' says he laughin', and shook my hand friendly. Me heart warmed to a countryman o' my own, and I was right sorry for him in the line's jaws.

'Get goin',' I advised him, 'if ever you want to see the Wicklow mountains again.'

'To-morrow,' says he, 'but I have another appointment to-day. I'm from the Dictation Machine Company.'

'What's that, in hell's name?'

'This is it,' says he, kneein' the cardboard box. 'A dictation machine. You talk into it, and, warble to retain, it talks back to the press of a button.'

'Are you after tellin' me—?'

'Listen brother! I am here by appointment to see A. H. Giles. Lead me to him, and hear me put it across. This is the machine as used by Egber Walters himself, and he grinds out six books a year with it—'

Hurroo!' says I. 'That's the line to take. Talk Egber to the gourilla, and you might escape with your life. Folly me, say an act of contrition, and God ha' mercy on your soul!'

So I led him round be the back of the stairs, an' kicked the dreaded door hard.

'Get to hell out o' that!' came the usual bellow, but all the same, a dot-and-carry shuffle came across the floor, and the door went flying open.

'Where's that dam' coffee—? Hids o' hell! Who did you let in this time?'

'The Dictation Machine Company by appointment,' strikes in the Irishman. 'My name is O'Broder—'

'Blast you and your name!' says A. H., true to form, and glared like a man-eater. Begod sir! O'Broder glared back, and after a while the ould fella set back

into the room and spoke a bit milder. 'All right!
Come in and let's see this machine that lays the golden
eggs. Like hell it does!'

'It laid six of them in one year for Egber Walters,'
comes in the bold O'Broder.

'You're a liar!' roars Giles. 'That dam' Walters
uses ghosts to turn out his balderdash.'

Ghosts! that's what he said. An' what would a
ghost use for pen and ink? Fire an' brimstone maybe!
Did you ever hear the like? I saw the lad's shoulders
stiffen, and be the look in his eye he was contimplatin'
his chances of climbing the big ape. He decided agin it,
for he spoke mild enough.

'The proof of the puddin' is atin' it,' says he. 'I
assure you, Mr Giles, this machine is the answer to the
best-seller—blah—blah—blah!' Like all them smart
salesmen he had a line o' talk to coax a bird off a
bough, but he hadn't two yards of it out of him till old
Giles stamped on into speechlessness.

'Cut the cackle and tackle the hosses!' he bawled.
'Show me what your confounded machine can do, an'
I'll give it a whirl. Get on with it!'

So I helped the salesman to get the black box out of
its case, and set it up on a corner of the desk. Then
he plugged the electric cable into the wall, and reached
into the case for a round flat plate that he called a wax
dixobolus. Oh! all right! A wax disc is it. Very good!
a wax dix, and he waved it in the air, and spills his
piece some more.

'Behould! you fit this di-disc in here, and take hold
of this inducing cable—' that was the limber wire pipe
with the mouth trumpet—and away with him to show

the tricks o' the trade. Flick a lever—forward—talk into the trumpet in an easy way of conversation—flick—reverse—listen in—press button—stop—let go, and on you go. A child could understand it.

After a while ould A. H. growled like a bulldog, shoved me out of his way, and made a grab at the speaking-tube.

'Let me try it, consarn you! Go on! turn the juice on.'

O'Broder began promptin' him careful, but the ould hulk lost the hinder-end of his patience, clapped the trumpet over a half-acre of ear, and let loose a stream of abased language.

O'Boder said nothing, but he reached for the trumpet and brought it round foreninst the ould fellow's gob; and the old fellow went on shoutin'. He was on a new book at the time, and he was recitin' a piece out of it. MacClinkey, his invetherate hero, was tongue-lashing a lascar member of the infayriour races for dropping an anchor on his corn or some little thing, and beglory, sir, me two ears went red—and I am used to langwidge, as you ought to know. He went on for a coupla minutes, and finished with the howl of a buck-wolf.

'If your gadget stands that, it'll stand hell's fire,' says he chucklin', 'let's hear it back!'

So O'Broder switched a lever, and clapped the trumpet over the old fellow's ear. Manalive! his wan eye lost itself atween crinkles an' the loose hulk of his body shivered with emotion.

'MacClinkey, you hoor, is it your own self?' he half whispered, awe and wonder in his voice. 'That's the stuff to give him, you whalp of a Glesca watherrat! Say that agin—that's good! Bingo bongo! and that settles him.'

All at once he was a new man, and pounded O'Broder with questions, but if he took in the answers, I don't know. And, then, he pointed at the disc.

'What'll it hold?'

'Two thousand words average, and after that as many discs as you want.'

'How many have you in that case?'

'A dozen for trial—that's our limit.'

I could see him doing the multiplication table in his head.

'Twenty four—or is it twenty six thousand?' says I.

'Four dozen discs for a full-length MacClinkey,' strikes in O'Broder, 'and you got Egber Walters tied to the ground.'

'Four dozen discs, and what do I do with them?' puts the old fella cute as a fox. And the Irishman was ready for him.

'Then, my good sir, if you prevail yourself of our Typing Service I collect the discs, and week after that I return you a correct and truly improper typescript of a novel ready to be printed.'

A. H. made up his mind then and there, and clapped wan hand on the other. 'Damme! you're on, and God ha' mercy on your soul! Send me another three dozen discs before the week-end, and come round yourself on Tuesday—no, make it Wednesday at five.' He shook a mighty fist. 'One or two things is bound to happen then. I'll pay you cash on the nail, or I'll take your Irish lude off in three operations. Get out o' here both of you! Out dam' you, out!' And he shoved and shooed us out of the room, and locked the door on himself.

O'Broder was a decent spud. At the front door he slipped me a half-note, and him as pleased as Punch and Judy.

'Keep an eye on the ould geezer,' says he, 'and we got him by the short hairs. Twenty quid commission for twenty minutes' work, and I need it. I'm catching the Night Mail for Dublin, and I'll be at Baldoyle Races for the Bank Holiday.'

'I wish I was with you,' says I, homesick.

'Two's company,' says he, a wink in wan eye.

'And is she nice?' I comes back.

'"A snowdrift neath a beechen bough her neck and nut-brown hair," as the song has it,' says he, and away with him down the path whistlin' like a lark in the clear air, as the other song has it.

Look at here now! I have worked hard and often in this garden and out of it, but the next four or five days beyant in Chiswick was the toughest time I ever rencountered. Not so much hard as tough, for I had no time for recuperation! The great A. H. Giles was in the throws of creations, an' my job was to supply the raw material for a head of steam.

Mind you, I never set eyes on him for four days. All I had to do was put a can of black coffee down on the door mat, and fill it up again when it was empty. Four days and four nights, and if I slept two hours at a time I was lucky, for his yowls would waken a dormouse.

Maybe he slept too, off and on. I don't know, but any time I woke up I could hear him shuffling and talking to the machine, or shouting abuse or laughter, or wheedling shamefully accordin' to the matter in hand. Four days and four nights, an' I was dead on my feet at the end of 'em, and it was then that I came to the judeecious conclusion, that meself and a dictation machine could not cohabit the same premises and live.

It was Tuesday evenin' about five that A. H. came out of his private hell. An' he come out spent to the last thread. His face was like a ploughed field, his wan eye was a burnt hole in a blanket, an' there was a growth like a furze bush from ear to ear. He wasn't sportin' a collar or tie or jacket or waistcoat, and his galluses was tied round his paunch. He frightened me, like a dead man walkin'.

He never opened his trap to me, but crawled up the stairs by haulin' on the bannister, and I heard water runnin' in the bathroom. In half an hour he was down again, dressed an' washed to meet legal requirements, but if anything he looked worse than ever in a 'masculated way.

'I'm going out for grup-pile,' he growled hoarse as a crow. 'Wait up for instructions.'

'Any particular place you'd like to be buried?' I says.

'Go to hell!' says he, and away with him.

I had a good sleep to myself in the front room, and he waked me up about midnight with the toe of his boot. I leapt up rearin'.

'If you wasn't in a rejooced condition I'd break you in three halves,' I challenged him, but he only shook his bull's head at me.

He wasn't more than two parts soaked, and I hadn't

no trouble in bestowing him to security on the divan couch. And the last thing he said was:

'Take that machine and discs to the front room, and hold that Irisher till I wake up. If he has to wait he can look over the machine for the second round.'

'That murderin' machine will save someone from hangin',' I tells him, and left him to his drames.

I slept a solid ten hours that night, and woke to a fine summer morning. The house was dead quiet for the first time in living memory. Ordinary days the floor would be lifting under me with howls from below.

I crept circumspect downstairs, an' had a peep round the door of the sanctorum, an' there he was on his back, his vamps protruding under a sheet, and his mouth wide catchin' flies. I left him at it and he slept on and on.

The house was so quiet all that day that it disturbed me, and for an hour at a time I cogitated the idee of slippin' out and losin' myself in the heart o' London. The old trouble, you know, was comin' on me, and I knew that I would never rest easy agin till I had an Irish road under my feet. But I raylinted in the end, for I wanted to see the O'Broder lad complete his sale. Hell, no! I was not anticipatin' another half-note.

He turned up at five prompt, and I met him at the door. He stopped grinnin' an' shook his head at me.

'My poor fella!' says he, 'you need a breath o' Wicklow air. Look what it done to me!'

There was fresh colour in his face, right enough, and the two eyes of him was sparklin' like plugs.

'Dublin makes a man of you, body and sowl,' says he. 'Lead me to your ooran-outang, an' I'll take his lith'rary style apart for you. He aint got any.'

'Come in!' says I in a cold way. 'Come on in, you manslaughterer!'

He reared back. 'Hell! he's not dead?'

'Sawin' wood like a Chinee, but on the road to hell all the same. Come on in!'

I took him into the front room, and he reared back again when he saw the devil's machine on a side-table.

'Me sainted aunt!' he squawked. 'Don't tell me he thrun it out?'

'Not him! He only wants you to vet the dam' thing for another round. You sold the poor white naygur down the river as sure as a gun. Take a look at them things over there!'

Over there on the side-board was four rack affairs in a row, an' each rack was slotted to hold an exact dozen of wax di-discs.

'Not the whole shootin' match—no man could in the time!' cried O'Broder constarnated.

'You can see for yourself,' I tells him. ' I dunno!'

He went across and looked over the racks, and nodded his head agreeable.

'Method in the ould boy's woolgatherin'!' he says, muttering. 'These here discs are all numbered rota- tively, and not a blank nowhere.' He picked out a disc and looked at it. 'Yep! this has been talked over, and by an expert.' He picked out another, and here and there and then the last one of all, and wonder come out on him as if he was perspirin'. 'My heavings!

My sowl in glory! My fear o' hell! close on a hundred thousan' words in less than a week! A full lengther from Dan to Bathsheeba, an' no holes barred. You were right, my Dublin Jackeen! I sold the white buck down the river.'

'Very good, Mister Simon hegroo!' I says. 'Collec' your blood-crusted cash, an' his death on your sowl forever and a day.'

And it was there I noticed a disturbance shadin' his face. He picked out a disc promiscu's and examined it this way and that, mutterin' away to himself. 'An expert I said, and an expert it is! Reg'lar as clockwork, and not a gouge anywhere. Gosh! he must have toned himself down as smooth as silk.'

'He wrastled the angel in the lord catch-as-catch-can ever since Holy Thursday,' I tells him, 'an' if there was silk anywhere it was a thing of shreds and patches like the song in the Mikydoo.'

Frowning away to himself, he came back to the machine, and slipped the disc on the turntable, moved the machine convanient, plugged it in, clapped the trumpet to his ear, and switched on.

Look sir! I thought his bottom jaw was fallin' off, and he had to use his free hand to restore it approximate; an' his eyes was no longer sparkin' but had the colour of skim-milk. An' he was speechless for the time. An' then, an' then, he tried another disc and another and the last disc of all; and the gloom went deeper and deeper into his gizzard. And by this time he was talking to himself like running water.

'Whatever are you sayin'?' I asks him.

'The act of contrition you told me to say Holy

Thursday,' says he, an' his bloody Irish temper began
to climb the pole. His eyes went glaring yellow, and
he put a fist under me nose.

'I told you, you adenoidal son of a Inchicore
boilermaker—I told you to keep an eye on him. Did
you?'

'Aisy!' says I, movin' outside a wallop in the puss.
'Aisy! you Wicklow protestantiser. I didn't see
nothing. He thrum me out—you saw him—an' locked
himself in for five days an' five nights. What in hell's
name did he do wrong anyway?'

He quietened then, for there was justice in him
somewheres.

'I know what he did, the supayrior Mr Giles,' he
says bitterly. 'Come here, and I'll show you!'

He dragged me across be the collar, put the trumpet
to my ear and switched the juice.

Listen to me now. I expected a bull's bellow to bust
the drum o' my ear. Not on your life. What I heard
was the sort of a hoarse whisper of a diamond point
scrapin' the wax, and an odd blast of foreign noise that
I reco'nised as ould Giles's voice comin' from a mile
off. Divil the thing else on the whole disc.'

'Holy Saint James's Street!' says I, swallowin' me
palate. 'Are they all like this one?'

'Without no shadow o' doubt.'

'God save us all! What'll he do? Oh, holy murdher,
what won't he do?'

'The question is what will I do?' says O'Broder.

'He'll never stand for five days of hell, and nothing
to show for it. He'll kill you stone cold dead.'

'Or I'll kill him, and I don't mind which.'

'You could run for it, couldn't you?' says I, temptin' him.

'I could,' says he, 'and laive the spiles behind.' And there he gave a heave to his shoulders, and climbed on top of his troubles, like all his breed. 'Ho-ho-ho! the slickest deal I ever put across, and it's down the drain. Ah well! Sure tomorrow is another day.'

'If we live to see it,' I warns him.

Just as you say,' he agrees, and looked at me in a considering way. 'Maybe you are right at that,' he said at last. 'Why not leave the old buxaneer champion in the forsaken field—and he can kill you if he wants too?' He cracked a finger and thumb. 'No use trying to squeeze spilled milk back into a clane jug. You take hold o' those crates, and I'll manhandle the machine.'

If we had two more minutes we'd ha' stole away like the Arabs of old, but the signs was agin us. A door banged to shake the house, and there was a shuffle o' bare feet outside in the passage. Then our door cracked to the wall, an' there was my outrageous old scarecrow leaning on the jamb. He had to lean, for he was only half awake an' half alive. He looked as old as a mountain, an' there was black valleys in the folds of his face. A rag of a silk dressing-gown was open to show a vi'lent pair of pyjamas, an' his bare feet was like a hawk's claws holding on to the floor.

'Back again!' he said hoarse as an ould rock. 'I got work for you, me lad. Is that machine in shape?'

O'Broder pulled himself up like a game cock, and then eased off again, an' judgin' by his face, I saw what was in his mind. He was lookin' at an old an' done man; a husk of a man with no corn in him any more, an' ould cock without a spur preten'in' to be lord on his own dunghill. The livin' young fellow shook his head sorrowfull.

'You'll not be needing that machine any more, Mr Giles,' he said, mild as buttermilk.

The ould fellow shuffled a step and a dot into the room, and balanced precar'ous. He let loose a wake bellow.

'Blunderin' wars! That's my machine till I say no. See them there discs—four dozen—a bleedin' record— and the best thing I ever done. Take 'em away and show me results, blast you!'

'You poor dumb old cluck,' says the O'Broder.

An' when he said that I got hould o' the sweepin' brush I had in a corner for self defence. The Irish lad had a good hold o' his risin' temper, an' the old fellow was dumbfoundered for the occasion.

'You poor dumb old cluck!' says O'Broder. 'You been boss of the infayriour races too long in foreign parts to listen to what another man tells you—you and your blatted MacClinkey. I belong to no infayriour race, Mr Giles, and what I says goes regarding this dictation machine. You didn't listen to me.'

'The thing was as straight as life an' death—I followed instructions—'

'Like hell you did!' O'Broder went over to the machine, an' picked up the speakin'-tube. 'This is what you did, Mr Giles. You held this mouthpiece over your ear and talked—'

'As you told me,' says Giles in a thin way.

'No, sir! I told you to hold it there close to your mouth and talk into it. Then you could listen in if you wanted to. For five days and five nights you held it there over your ear and shouted into empty air.' His voice rose, and he pointed a hand. 'If you must know, there's not a single solitary artic'late word raycorded on them there discs.'

Giles set back one, two, four steps an' sat down with a thump on me own particular chair. His one eye was i'noble with consternation.

'No raycord at all?' he said down in his windpipe.

'Not a single artic'late word,' said O'Broder again.

The ould boy was up against a stone wall for the first time in his life. He put his head in his palms, an' a groan came up from the pit of his stomach.

'I know I was a dam' fool to play with a new gadget,' he said hollow like.

'Forget it, Mr Giles—if you can,' said O'Broder in a quiet way. 'We'll cancel the whole thing, and I'll take the machine out of your sight.'

Ould Giles kept his eyes covered, but moved his thumb. 'Don't let me see it again—or I'll kill someone,' he whispered.

O'Broder handled the machine, and nodded me towards the racks. And do you know, the ould hayro had the last word. It was at my back going out the door.

'Come back!' says he. 'Come back and dig your own grave.'

That was me dismiss. I didn't come back. Ould Giles could never face me again on level terms, an' if I as much as moved a hand towards me ear he'd try

to kill me. I got a lift from O'Broder as far as the
Strand, and in two days I had the roads of Wicklow,
Wexford, Waterford, and Kilkenny under me two
round feet. I never set eyes on A. H. Giles again. And
that's my story for you.

. . . . .

I contemplated Thomasheen James, and he met my
gaze with a guilefully guileless eye.

'You didn't see Giles again,' I said. 'But have you
seen this O'Broder?'

Thomasheen James flung a careless hand. 'Sure,
oh sure! Frequent and free! He's in Dublin these years,
head manager for his firm in all Ireland. A friendly
man, and a gallant wife.' The old wistful look was in
his eye. 'A brown-haired woman with a lustry eye,
an' a pleasant word for me any time I call on them
beyant in Mount Merrion. "Tommy boy, draw a cork
for yourself while I butter a sangwich." An' a half
dollar slipped into the heel o' my fist by the man of
the house.'

'When did you see him last?' I pursued the inquisition.

'Let me see now!' He considered deeply. 'Was it
last night, or ere last night, or the night before?
Anyway, he stood me a pint in Bolan's Bar. And do
you know this? For some reason beyant me compri-
hendin' he's a great admirer of your works o' pure
fiction. Says he to me, "But why don't he write more?
A book every coupla year is no output at all, an' he
could easy double it with no natural exertion." So
he said whatever.'

'And so he set you to canvas me for a dictating machine?'

'He did not, begobs!' he denied warmly. 'I wouldn't never do it.' His tone changed. 'But if he was to call on you in a friendly way in about an hour's time, you wouldn't be stuck be no blind pig in a poke.'

'If he brings a dictating machine inside that gate,' I said firmly, 'I'll kick it into smithereens.'

'Hurroo! the very thing,' applauded Thomasheen James. 'Wasn't the whole subject o' me story leadin' you that direction. Look! If you was to give me the Bank in Ireland I wouldn't again cohabit the wan primises with a dictation machine.'

Thomasheen James is still on the premises. But perhaps I should state that this is the first story I have dictated into one of my friend O'Broder's machines.

WHY SHOULD I SIT AND SIGH?

I

THEY were a young couple, not six months married, and they should have been as happy as the day was long; and the day was long, for it was in the very heart of June: a slumbrous Sunday in June, early in the afternoon, with a gentle warmth in the sun and a tenuous haze over the orange glory of the furze on all the hillsides.

The thatched cottage nestled securely half-way up the slope at the head of a small valley. A hundred paces below, a spring bubbled from the limestone roots of the hill into a miniature pool fenced in by flat slabs of lichened rock; and the overflow went singing down the hollow between clumps of sally and bracken. And far away, in a deep notch of the mountains, the Atlantic sea shimmered under the sun.

Maire Dhue—dark-haired Mary—sat on a straw hassock at the hearthside where the remnants of a peat fire were deeply smoored in white ashes. She was a long-limbed young woman who, later on, would be a veritable matron and matriarch: nobly busted, placid-eyed, with long strong bones padded in firm flesh. She was knitting placidly, unhurriedly, and, sometimes, she smiled softly at a thought of her own.

Manus Boy—Yellow Magnus—sat on a rush-bottomed chair at the other side of the fire; his face was solemn and hard as justice, his eyes, unseeing, looking through the open door across the valley, and the rich sombre yellow of his eyes matching the golden glory of the furze over there. He was feeling his first touch of discontent, and he was frightened as well as unhappy.

He was a man of no more than middle height, but mighty shouldered, deep-chested, flat-flanked, with a bush of yellow hair and a lean aquiline face, eagle-eyed. And, for the first time, he felt chained like a chained eagle. He was wearing easy fitting grey flannels, and his open-necked white shirt showed the splendid golden column of his neck.

Maire lifted slow blue eyes, and looked at her husband—a long deep considering look—and then she smiled wisely, as a woman will, old or young, but there was a trace of wistfulness in her smile too. She spoke, as if to herself, in her soft western voice.

'So it has come, then.'

'What has come then?' There was a quick startle in her husband's voice.

'What my mother told me to look for—sooner than I thought, my sorrow!' Maire's voice half-mused.

There was a resonant timbre in Manus's voice, and he made it deeper.

'A wise man told me one time that a wife's mother is apt to be an interfering woman. I believe it.'

'Not my mother,' said Maire, and went on in the same quiet strain, as if musing to herself. 'She told me that a live man and him married would be feeling the halter in the first year.'

'Whatever are you talking about?' Manus wanted to know, though well he knew.

Maire gave him her slow direct gaze. 'You are a live man, Manus Boy, and you were lively too, a rag on many a bush, a seeing man, and a doing man, and your hand on more than one girl. And now you feel tied and bound and spancelled to a strange woman's daughter.'

'You are my wife, whoever your mother is,' said Manus gruffly.

Maire went on equably. 'Man that you are, you will have to get over it in your own way, for myself can't help you; but if you don't get over it that will be God's will too—or my blame, for I have not yet the power over you.'

'Who is to blame, you foolish girl?' Manus chided.

Maire put her knitting aside, and leant towards the long-thighed tongs. 'Leave it be, Boy,' she said cheerfully enough. 'Look! I'll light a furze root from the embers, and we'll make a cup of tea to ourselves. It is a comforting thing tea, and might restore you for a short while. Will you go down to the spring for a pail of fresh water?'

'I will, and welcome,' said Manus, promptly on his feet. Any excuse to get into the open by himself away from those wise blue eyes! He picked up the zinc-hooped wooden pail from below the dresser of brown delf, and bent below the lintel into the drowsy sunlight.

'Don't be more than an hour, anyway,' Maire called after him.

'Five minutes and I'll be back,' Manus called over his shoulder.

'Mother-o'-God, send him back to me—all of him!' prayed Maire, and her voice was no longer equable.

126

2

Manus Boy, head and shoulders adroop, and the pail hanging loose from a lax hand, went down the slope over flat stone shelves between furze and bracken clumps. He walked a little bow-legged, and though he slouched lazily, there was about him a sense of controlled virility that he might explode at any moment.

The pool was only twenty feet across, and not more than two feet deep, and it was bottomed with white pebbles. The water was so crystal clear that it would be invisible only for the faint tremors that kept flowing across it from the intake trickle under a shelf of limestone.

Manus put the pail down on a flat slab close to the water. A circle had been worn on the surface of the slab by the many pails that had rested there over the centuries. He thrust his hands deep into his pockets, looked down-headed into the crystal wimpling, and sighed deeply. Gloom was in him and around him. After a while he moved a step aside, and sat himself on a knee-high boss of rock, and after another while he shook his yellow head and murmured deeply to himself.

'It is true for her; indeed it is true for her, and dam' her mother's eyes! Tied to the one woman all my life! Oh! the times that were, the great times that were—and the times that will never come again, for, bad as I am, there's an honest streak in me. . . . I do, I must love that girl up there, but it is a tame love now, and no wild ecstacy any more. But I'll get used to that too, and grow sluggishly content. . . . And she will be the mother of my sons, and hold me in one place stagnant as a rain-splash in a rut, and as the sun dries the splash, so will age dry me, and I'll be old bones at the fire corner over against an ageing woman. Never again the loose foot and the woman not kissed before, never again rain on the brae and the wind blowing. Heigh-ho ! . . .'

It was then, in the heart of that mood, that a strange waiting hush came about Manus. The tinkle of the inlet runlet, the sighing song of the streamlet down the valley grew remote as in a dream ; no bird sang in these dead hours of the day, the goldfinches no longer flitted from whin to whin, no rook flapped lazily along the slopes. Everything was hushed and waiting.

And then a new sound got through to Manus in his remoteness. It was the sound of someone or something softly splashing the water at the end of the pool not ten feet away ; and the water now flowed ripple after ripple. Manus let his eyes drift, and what he saw stilled his heart and changed his mood utterly.

It was if a wand had touched him ; it was as if the solid land of Ireland about him had become unreal and without substance ; it was as if himself and what his eyes saw were in a dimension of their own in a dream world. He was under a spell, though he did not know it.

What his eyes saw were a pair of shapely small feet, toes spread and lifted, softly churning the water. They were creamy-white feet, pink-toed, and an entrancing blue vein went delicately aslant an instep into the curve of an ankle. The old devil, never far under the surface, lifted head in Manus, and the skilly use of words had not forsaken him. The voice in his throat was as vibrant as a bell.

'They are made to tread on a man's heart, and the heart wanting more torment.'

And a silver mocking voice made answer:

'So it has been said.'

'Ay! and an ankle like that I once saw in a dream.'

'That dream I made you dream.'

His hand moved in an upward curve.

'And that gentle, slender, flowing line—'

A mellow tinkle of laughter stopped him.

'That is as far as you need go, golden man.'

'But one could be thinking,' said Manus softly.

He lifted eyes then, and was pleased by what he saw.

She was a brown girl and dainty: shining brown in the hair, lustrous brown in the eyes, golden tanned in neck and breast and slender arms, and the delicate blood dusky in her cheeks to the caress of his eyes. She was wearing a low-necked, short-sleeved, flowing diaphanous dress the colour of ripe corn, with a loose-ended wide sash of a deeper shade studded with topaz, and her brown hair was held loosely by a wheaten ribbon.

The whole blending of her colours and colouring gave her an extraordinary vividness, a strange other-world vividness. Her eyes sparkled at him, her mouth smiled at him, showing the tips of small white teeth, and her smile was of heart-stirring sweetness and extraordinary gaiety, a gaiety of time-out-of-mind, a gaiety outside time and space.

Manus smiled back at her, and lifted a sweeping arm in salute.

'Under your feet, Princess.'

She crowed delightedly. 'Princess! But that is my name. How did you know, golden man?'

'What other name could you have in all the world?' said Manus.

'And your own name, it is Golden?'

'I am known as Manus Boy, which means Yellow Magnus.'

'Not yellow! Golden, golden! Golden is your name.'

'Whatever you say, Princess,' said Manus agreeably.

She, in one deft motion, swung her feet aside out of the water and under the billowing hem of her dress. Then she leant aside on one brown hand, and contemplated Manus seriously. But the seriousness was not genuine.

'You did not live in this place always, Golden?' she put to him then.

'Not always, Princess. That is our—my summer cottage up the slope.'

'A good choice for summer.'

'Surely,' said Manus complacently. 'For in this choice place I meet a princess, and besides, it is the sweetest valley in all the west.'

Again her laughter mocked him and she shook her head so that her brown hair swung from one shoulder to the other.

'No—no! not the sweetest. The valley where I live—my Queen-mother's valley—is the loveliest of all the valleys.'

'It will be some distance away,' said Manus politely.

'It is but over there.' She lifted a curving arm and

softly stabbed a finger southwards. 'Over that small hill it is and nowhere other.'

Manus knew that over that small hill was a wilderness of stone outcrops in a broken country of moorland spreading twenty miles to the Mountains of Maam. He had shot and hunted over it, and there was no valley in it anywhere. He made judicious answer.

'Where you live, Princess, such a valley would be.'

She shook her head at him, and grimaced in impish pretended anger. 'You do not believe, you do not believe me. But it is there, there.' Again she swung her arm and stabbed a finger. 'Up the valley and through the gap, and there is my valley below you.' She was impulsive now. 'Look! let me show you. I dare you to let me show you. Come!'

She lifted off the stone lightly as a bird, slipped her feet into flat brown sandals, and flitted to him tip-toe, her left hand out. He was already on his feet, and his right hand accepted her left. The soft coolness of her palm went up his arm and turned to heat in his throat.

And the two of them hand in hand went down the hollow of the little valley by the stream. It was as easy as that.

He never looked back, never looked up towards the house where his young wife waited for her pail of spring water. In his present mood that old tame life was as dim and unsure as a dream remembered.

A bare quarter mile down the valley a gap opened in the slope to the left, and to the draw of her hand he turned in with her. Manus knew that gap. It finished in a steep chorrie of boulders, and he had often been up and over into the wild country beyond.

They came to the face of the chorrie, but did not climb. She drew him to the right along the front of it, where, as he knew, was only a bounding wall of stone. He was wrong, for there was now a narrow opening between chorrie and cliff that he had not noticed before but that did not surprise him in the least. Through that opening she led him, in and on and up and up, in a half-shade, the rock walls towering on either hand, and the sky far overhead.

And then the gorge widened, the walls lowered, and, after one final stiff pinch, they came out into the open at the head of the pass. There the little eager pressure of her palm halted him.

3

'Look, oh look!' She was on tip-toe and tugging at his hand. 'That is my very own valley where my mother reigns.'

'I knew in my heart it was there all the time,' said Manus deeply.

'And beautiful?'

'There is no small valley anywhere so beautiful.'

The valley that he had forsaken had now no objective reality in his mind, but this new valley was solidly real. It was a big, bowl-shaped green hollow in the hills. The green ran up into brown slopes that rolled over smoothly, and, behind, rose other slopes a fainter brown, and, behind these, other slopes turning purple, and, behind all, the smoky blue ghosts of mountains. And arching above all beyond all was a high far-flung blue sky full of soft sunlight.

There was a small lake in the flat bottom of the bowl, with a cascade splashing in at one end and a stream flowing out like a shining ribbon at the other. There were wide demesnes sweeping round the lake, clumped with flowering shrubs, and, between the clumps, fallow-deer and roe-deer and gazelles browsed and romped. To the left of the lake was a spread of lawn, emerald green with a border brilliant with the flowers of summer; and at the back of the lawn on a high terrace stood a long, wide, low, lime-white mansion, with a scarlet many-gabled roof acres wide.

But, most important of all, there were many people on the lawn and about the lake, scores and scores and scores of people of both sexes clothed in all the colours and blends of the rainbow; some were reclining on the grass, some slouching on seats of marble, some strolling with linked arms, many running about at some ball game, and many swimming and splashing in the lake, bodies white shining; and two tall fellows were wrestling actively in a ring of onlookers whose cheering mocking voices came up the slope thin and high as the skirling of gulls.

'That is my Queen-mother's great house,' said Princess, finger apoint, 'and these her people and my dear friends.'

'Jealous I might be of one here and there,' said Manus.

'Jealous! That is a word I do not know. Is it love?'

'The obverse of the medal, brown darling. But you will have love in this delectable place? It is a subject I could tell you about.'

'Yes, yes, yes! Love and more love. In this valley there is nothing but love and gaiety.'

'Love is not often gay, but I might be jealous all the same,' Manus told her.

She released his hand now, and slipped an arm inside his elbow.

'Golden dear,' she said, softly persuasive, 'you will come down and kiss the Queen's hand, and meet my friends?'

'What you want me to do, that I will do,' said Manus.

'My dear one,' she whispered softly.

So they moved down leisurely over the grassy slopes and between fragrant shrubs, and talked and talked—and it was still afternoon, a land in which it seemed always afternoon.

'Are you a champion, Golden?' she asked him.

'Your champion, Princess.'

'But a great champion?'

'There might be one or two greater,' said Manus carelessly.

'And you fight other champions?'

'I have used my hands,' Manus told her, and that was true.

'And a wrestler?'

'A bit collar-and-elbow in the days of my youth.'

'Our champions are great champions, Golden.'

'I will challenge them for you one after the other,' said Manus.

'No—no!' There was a serious note in her voice for the first time. 'There is one, the greatest, the greatest in all the valleys—'

'There are other valleys?'

She swung an arm gracefully wide. 'Valleys without number, and the greatest champion of all is our champion, Cuchulain.'

'There was, indeed, a great hero of that name.'

'He is here now.'

'And you love him?'

'There is love always.'

'I will take a look at your Cuchulain,' said Manus soberly.

'But no!' she was urgent. 'He would break you in two with his hands.'

He pressed her arm inside his, and nudged her softly with his shoulder. 'Same as I could break you with my hands?'

'Your dear, ugly, brown hands! they are round my heart already.' There was a thrill in her voice, and his blood answered it.

So they moved down to the easier slopes, and were seen coming; and many, crying gay, shrill greetings, came flocking, multi-coloured, to meet them. The maidens came first, skipping and holding hands, and swung in an eager laughing ring around them. They were all daintily lovely, and of all colourings, and shimmerings, but to Manus's mind, none of them had the extraordinary vividness of his Princess. Already he felt possessive.

The men in richer colours, like a garden of peacocks, came more slowly, bustled through the ring of maidens, and faced the two, thrusting heads forward and grimacing at Princess with a ferocity that Manus recognised as make-believe. Himself they ignored for the present.

But Princess brushed them aside with a quick imperious gesture, and cried:

'Children, first my Queen-mother.'

The crowd swung in behind, and laughed and chattered and wondered about this soberly-clad, deep-chested, yellow-eyed stranger who radiated controlled power, and had a sombre gravity that they could not assess. And one whispered to another. 'Would this hero have what is called a soul?'

Manus and Princess, still arm in arm, skirted round the lake and came up between flower-beds to the wide lawn, where the rest of the company made a curve back of a white marble dais whereon a malachite canopy enclosed a wide throne-seat of white marble piled with blue and yellow cushions. And among the cushions sat a great lady, a tiara of gold and jewels in her yellow hair.

A golden, noble, mature woman she was, but not old. Indeed, in that valley Manus never met an old man or an ageing woman. Nor did he meet any children.

Princess still holding his arm, Manus mounted the steps of the dais slowly and gravely, and Princess cried out eagerly:

'Queen-mother Fand, I present my new champion, Golden.'

Queen-mother bent her fine head and smiled slowly.

'Your new champion is welcome here, little one.' Her voice was low pitched where all the other voices were high and even shrill. And Manus noticed, too, that she was a quiet woman, and grave, and that behind her slate-blue eyes was something that might be melancholy, as if she half knew something precious and would never know the other half. She reached him a slow hand at the end of a moulded arm, and Manus took the coolness of it in his finger-tips and bent his lips to it. And Princess made exultant little boast:

'All by myself I found him Queen-mother.'

'You found him when the mood was on him and the gate open, my daughter,' said the woman wisely. 'He is a quiet man, your champion.'

'But he can speak Mother Fand, and his words have a hidden meaning.'

'You may find out that meaning if you hold him long enough.'

Princess threw up her hands joyously, and cried:

'I will keep him forever and ever and ever.'

'That has been tried before,' said the woman, a sad mockery in her voice. 'Go now to your friends and rivals!'

There is no need to go into details. The slow afternoon passed into evening, and evening into gloaming, but at no time did darkness come. Manus, Princess ever at his side, strolled here and there and talked to this one and that one; he looked on at the games and wrestling and make-believe fighting, and once he swam in the lake, outpacing Princess and most of the others. When he came out of the water he found that his grey flannels had disappeared, and in their place were a gorgeous silken tunic and trews of venetian red, with a corn-coloured sash studded with topaz. It was Princess's own sash to show whose champion he was. After some hesitation he donned his splendours, and was not even ashamed.

4

Sometime in the evening Princess whispered to him, a shade of doubt in her voice.

'It is the custom, Golden, for a new champion to show his skill. What are you skilled in besides love?'

From what he had seen, the young men were deft at wrestling, but merely playful at boxing, which was his own game. They were tall enough and active, but not durable looking, and he felt that a solid right hook might knock any one of them into the middle of next week—any of them except one.

'You will choose a wrestler for your poor champion,' he told her.

'That I will do,' she said eagerly, for I will not have you hurt. She put her hand over her heart and frowned. 'There is a strange feeling here when I think of it. You will let me choose, Golden please? You have a devil in your eyes.'

Holding his hand, she hopped lightly, skirts awhirl, on to a marble bench, and he stepped firmly up to her side. He was not a tall man, but her brown head was only level with his shoulder.

She clapped her hands and gave a clear, ringing halloo; and the young people came thronging as if knowing what was afoot. She reached a hand so that the back of it touched Manus's breast, and the silver of her voice carried far:

'This is now my champion, Golden, and he challenges one of you to wrestle—'

A mighty shout drowned her voice, and the youths

138

pressed forward, hands up, voices pealing, faces fierce, but gaiety in every eye.

'Try me! Try me! Try me!'

Princess's flat-handed imperious gesture brought silence, and she looked them over to choose a victim. Manus's voice was in her ear, his arm across her shoulder.

'Is the hero Cuchulain amongst them?'

'No, no, not Cuchulain,' and again, her hand came to her heart.

'That is he standing apart?'

'Yes, but he would break you in his hands, that hero. Look, Golden, dear!' and her voice was urgent and wistful, 'if you are shamed, I cannot stand the pain, and I might not have life in me any more.'

Manus was not heeding her. He had his eye on this Cuchulain for some time. A man in purple and red, he stood behind the crowd, feet wide-planted, hands on hips, and black head forward; a quiet man mostly serious where no one else was: dark in the hair, clearly pallid in face, blue-black in the eyes, not any taller than Manus, but wide as a door.

Manus found a dominance rise in him, not for the first time. He patted Princess's shoulder.

'Your champion chooses the best always, and after that works down to his own level. Stay and see!'

He moved aside her hands that would clutch him and took a long stride off the bench. And Princess stood there forlornly, her shoulders narrowed, and a constriction about her heart that her hands could not ease.

Manus strode straight at the press and shore through.

Something in the carriage of his head, some other-world savagery in his eyes made these young men move hastily aside to give him room.

And there he was, yellow-head thrown back and yellow eyes half hooded, face to face with Cuchulain. For the first time there was a hush over all that place.

Cuchulain smiled gravely, but Manus was nowhere near smiling. He was brusque.

'Are you that Cuchulain who was once the Hound of Ulster?'

'What I once was I do not know,' said Cuchulain, heavy voiced, 'but what I am now is well known.'

'The champion of all the valleys?'

'That is what I am.'

'Or the second best?'

'You would dispute it?' Cuchulain smiled again, but a spark lit behind the black eyes. 'I warn you that sometimes I lose my temper, and am rougher than is permitted. You will forgive me.'

'I might be rough too,' said Manus, 'and I will not ask anyone to forgive me.'

He thrust his right hand out low and his left high. Cuchulain did the same, and forthwith the two champions grappled. Slowly, link by link they took the strain, testing each other's strength before trying any feints or clips. And there Manus got the surprise of his life.

Cuchulain was indeed strong, weightily strong, but, somehow, there was no pith in him, no driving force, no explosive energy of body or soul to oppose the electric explosiveness of a man. He strained heavily, eyes hot and hotter, but Manus held him glued to the ground so that he could not flex a knee or flick a foot.

'Let us try it this way,' said Manus then. He loosed a spurt of energy, swung Cuchulain in half circle, and brought him down on spread feet; and in turn he took Cuchulain's sluggish swing and came down poised. And so at it they went, in half-swings, three-quarter swings, full swings, here and there about the lawn, Manus gradually increasing the tempo, so that the young people, crying shrilly, had to scatter and get out from under.

And then, with a sudden resistant wrench Manus brought that bear-like dance to a dead stop; and Cuchulain's legs buckled and he went down on his knees. But Manus brought him upright again, patted his shoulder, and let him go.

'Show you a trick or two sometime, brother,' Manus said, and walked away.

Everyone there knew that there was a new champion amongst them, and everyone cheered mightily, forgetting the defeated. But one tall fellow in green wanted to make sure. He sprang in front of Manus, and offered the wrestler's grip.

'You could not do that to me, new champion?' he challenged.

'This is for you,' said Manus, caught him forcefully by the shoulders, twirled him once, twice, thrice, and let him go; and the fellow went round like a teetotum, voice gagging, and finally fell flat on his face, grasping at the grass to keep the world from tilting.

And Manus walked on, laughter all round him, to where Princess waited on her bench, her eyes glistening with something that might be moisture. He lifted arms to her, and she came down into them, and she knew that she was being kissed—for the first time. Her heart would not let her speak.

What is the use of going on. It was evening now, the evening that never darkened, and there was feasting in the white palace, where rose-pink silken curtains moved in the soft air, and countless mirrors made endless crystal vistas. There were piled richly coloured fruits of all kinds, and curious and tantalising confections, and a light heady wine of two flavours, but there were no meats.

Thereafter there was music-making on harps and thin-sounding pipes, and arabesque-like dancing, and poetry-reciting and song-making and song-singing, and more feasting and dancing and singing, and Manus sang the one song he wanted to sing, an old passionate song, in his flexible baritone voice:

'I burn with drouth, O Strange Woman's Daughter!
Give me strong wine of love, not cool spring water,
Not pallid joy—red love and its sorrow,
For my heart you hold in hour hands' hollow.'

He sang that song for one only, and that one knew.

Need it be said. Manus did not go home that night. He did not even remember that he had any home to go to. And after that night he did not want to go anywhere.

He stayed a week, he stayed a month, he stayed a year. He stayed. And his brown Princess was always with him, and always loving him; and her Queen-mother, who had acquired wisdom somewhere, some-time, looked on, and smiled sadly.

It was an ideal life—maybe; an unending spiral of

enjoyment and games and thrills. Unending! Some might call it heaven. There were even wars of sorts between this valley and that valley: clangorous, shouting, wide-swinging battles, in which mighty blows were struck, and heroes strutted, and champions satisfactorily tumbled. And Manus was the champion of all the valleys. But blood! Was blood shed at all? For at the end of a strenuous day, Manus could not remember any hero lying stark in red gore.

5

It was sometime in the seventh year that the change of mood came over Manus. Make-believe gaiety, make-believe war began to weary him, and he began to move about by himself on the northern slopes of the valley, avoiding even Princess, in whose company there was a spell no longer. The scene, the people, the spiral of fevered pleasure-seeking were losing a sense of reality; and some inner vision was seeing a clear and wholesome world starkly etched under an evening sun. And there was a dark woman. . . . Oh God!

Princess noted his mood from the very beginning; she saw it bud and burgeon and bloom, and keep on blooming, and a new pain grew and grew in her. But she did not importune him, and some new desolate mood in herself would not let her do what she could do to hold him. She just followed him about at a distance, a woebegone small Princess, no longer shimmering with vividness, gay never again.

Came the day when Manus, heavy with gloom, sticky with the soft warmth no longer salubrious, plunged into the lake, battled sullenly against the clinging waters, and came out unrefreshed. He reached for his venetian reds. They were not there. There, instead, were the grey flannels that he had not seen or thought about for seven years. The roughish texture of them was pleasant to the feel, to his hands, to his legs, to the column of his neck; and the very stiffness of them, compared with silk, was oddly comforting and manly.

Again and heavy footed he plodded up the northern slopes, where no longer, as he well knew, was there a gap leading anywhere—anywhere he wanted to be. Gay voices called after him to join in a game of hurling, but to him they were only voices calling in a dream.

Princess watched him go, and herself went to where her Queen-mother sat, as usual, amongst her cushions; and that wise woman moved her fine blonde head from side to side.

'So it has come, little one,' she murmured sadly.

'And what now Queen-mother?'

'If you want your Golden, he can be held.'

'I want him.'

'There are spells—'

'And spells?'

'And more and more spells.'

'And when he wakes one time, any time, will he want to stay with me for myself, myself only?'

Queen-mother again moved her head slowly. 'There is a tie that no spell can kill forever. Listen, little one! You have the one chance that few get in all the valleys, but the pain is too great. Once, long ago, I too had that chance. I let my lover go, but you his daughter I could not forsake even to win a soul. I know only the half-life, but I know all the pain, and that pain I will not let you suffer. I will make a spell.'

Princess threw her head up, and her voice was anguished but deep.

'No, no, no! I am used to pain, and I will have no more spells.'

She turned away, and she too moved northwards, her feet unsure and her eyes blinded.

Manus sat on a shelf of stone close up to the northern rim of the valley. He was not slouching hopelessly. Though his head was down, his shoulders were held stiffly, and his arms folded firmly across his breast. And he was thinking.

'This is not life: it is only an image of life. Effort is useless, for effort leads nowhere, and all motion returns on one spiral. It is, maybe, some subtle form of hell. No, not hell! It is life without a soul, and I will have no more of it though I am held here forever. I threw my life away in a blind and selfish hour, the only life worth living. With manhood on you choose your road and hold by it. Take a wife and cleave to her, and to hell with romantic urges! Work and beget and rear and teach and toil. Leave hostages to fortune, let love renew itself as it will; and let one die unafraid. Oh, love that I threw away in a dark hour! Oh, my dark love! . . .

A whisper, that he did not know was a whisper, came out of the air.

'And she was beautiful?'

145

'That is only a word,' he whispered back. 'She had black hair and blue eyes, a generous mouth, and a white nape to her neck. No, not white! White is the colour of dread. A smooth and fragrant ivory! And when I used move my hand up from her neck through her hair, her hair used crackle and crisp between my finger, and the waves of it reached my throat.

'And she had the thing we call a soul?'

'Shining through in day and dark.'

'Ayeh me! there is no soul in this valley or in any valley. It is what we seek, and we do not know what it is. My Queen-mother knows, and she tells a story that once in a hundred years one of us wins a soul through great pain and great sacrifice, and that one is seen no more, ever. I held you as long as I could, Golden.'

'You held me a long time.'

'Not against your will?'

'Not against my will.'

'And I will not hold you against your will now. Pain I know, and if I must know more I will know it. Come!'

He found himself on his feet, her left hand holding his right as of yore. Head down he went where she drew him. He found himself in a gap of the hills going downwards; he found himself in shade between high stone walls, he found himself through the gut, and a clean cool live air in his face. And there was a final whisper.

'You are back now, Golden, and I go, where I do not know. All I know is that I will never see you again, never, never, never.'

6

After a while he had grace enough to lift his head and turn round. Princess was not there, and there was no longer a gap between the chorrie and the cliff. Stone piled on stone shouldered close against the retaining wall.

'And that is the end of that,' he said in his throat, and there was neither sorrow nor regret in him.

He went out of the side-gap then, and into his own valley, and up by the course of the runlet. He went slow-footed, heart down, head down, not able to lift his head, not daring to lift his head for fear of what he might see: ruined thatch, gaping windows, broken walls—or, worse, children, not his, playing about the half-door.

So in time he came to the little pool of spring water, and sat him down on the boss of stone where he had sat seven years before. He looked through the shimmering translucency of the water, and went deep into the recesses of his own mind.

It was again a sun-hazed summer afternoon, and stillness was over all that land. The birds were not yet singing, though goldfinches flitted from whin to whin; and the tinkle of running water was in a remote dimension of its own.

After a time Manus sighed deeply, drew in a long breath and stiffened his shoulders. The murmur of his voice was sad but not forlorn:

Seven years is a long time, but it is by, and there is nothing I can do about it. I threw the living life away, but there is great life in me still. If it be so willed, and

the one woman remains to me still, I will seek her out
at the world's end, and put my hands under her feet,
and cherish her, and strive for her and her children,
so that life shall be always eager and always calling.
And if that is not given me, as God made me, I will
face whatever life there is.'

He shook his head, fiercely resolute, looked about
him, and stared.

'That is a strange thing,' he said. 'It looks like our
water-pail, but our pail will be worn into staves these
many days.'

A zinc-hooped wooden pail did indeed rest on the
flag where many a pail had worn a ring. It was a good
new pail, and there were traces of moisture in the
bottom of it.

Manus held his breath, and, for the first time, looked
up the slope. Then he exhaled shortly. For the cottage
was still there, nestling securely into the breast of the
hill. It had not changed at all. The small four-paned
windows shone; the walls were still blue-white; the
door was still open to the summer air, but he could not
see inside; and the rough-cast chimney out of the
brown thatch sent up a thin ribbon of smoke, as if
some housewife were burning furze roots to boil a
kettle.

Manus smiled, and some of the old dare-devil was
back in his smile. He got to his feet.

'Whatever woman is in that house,' said he, 'she
will be having use for a pail of spring water. Very
well so! A pail of spring water she shall have, and
let it be a good beginning to set my feet on the seeking
road.'

Firmly, then, he scooped the pail full, and faced the upward path steadily, shelf above shelf amongst the furze and bracken. He stood in the open doorway, and his heart hollowed out, and he drew thin air into a tightened throat.

Maire, his young wife, sat there at the fireside on her hassock. She was placidly knitting, and a last furze-root was burning down into white ash. She half-turned and smiled her slow smile.

'You took a long time to bring me my pail of water,' she said in her quiet soft voice.

His voice might have broken if he had not kept it vibrating deeply in his throat.

'But in the end I brought it. Was it a long time, indeed?'

'A full hour, anyway.'

'I thought it was longer,' said Manus evenly.

'No. You were sitting on the stone hunched over, and brooding away to yourself. I thought you were asleep.'

'Asleep and dreaming. But at end—in one hour or in seven years—I had only one desire in all the world.'

Something in his voice, something in his eyes, made her heart shake her.

'Yes, Manus?' she said softly.

His voice thickened. 'I only wanted to come back to you and put my hands under your feet.'

Her heart turned completely over and her blue eyes were drowned in the glow of his yellow ones.

'Manus Boy, Manus Boy! You are back to me.'

'Till time and tides are done, one woman.'

He put the pail down at the fireside. He ran his

hand from the soft cream of her neck into her black hair, and it crisped and crinkled between his fingers. He bent his cheek to hers and whispered:

'Let us not boil the kettle for a small while yet.'

And she turned her mouth to his.

.   .   .   .   .

But what of the Fairy Princess? Was she only the vision of an hour to show a man the definite road he must take? It could be. Yet there is a tradition in that countryside of a sad and lonesome small song that comes out of the hillside in the gloaming of a June evening. Words have been put to that song, and here are a few of them:

'Why should I sit and sigh
    Pu'in bracken, pu'in bracken?
Why should I sit and sigh
    All alone and weary?'

It is not easy to win a soul.